Humiliation

STORIES

✦

Paulina Flores

Translated from the Spanish by
Megan McDowell

ONEWORLD

A Oneworld Book

First published in Great Britain, the Republic of Ireland and Australia
by Oneworld Publications, 2019

Originally published in Spanish as *Qué vergüenza* by Hueders, 2015

ISBN 978-1-78607-503-1
eISBN 978-1-78607-504-8

Printed and bound in Great Britain by Clays Ltd, Elcograf S.p.A.

Oneworld Publications
10 Bloomsbury Street
London WC1B 3SR
England

For Elizabeth

International Praise for *Humiliation*

'*Humiliation* is a brilliant book that captures the volatility of misunderstandings, the moment when failures matter less than the need to share them.'

Alejandro Zambra, award-winning author of *Ways of Going Home* and *Multiple Choice*

'A debut that marks the arrival of a powerful figure in Chilean literature... We must celebrate it wholeheartedly.'   *La Vanguardia*

'Every once in a while, one encounters a new voice and thinks: they will last... One of the best books of the year.'   *El País*

'The magic of Paulina Flores' writing lies in placing us in that critical moment when everything is about to change, yet everything seems still. A finely tuned literary high-wire act if ever there was one.'

Carlos Fonseca, author of *Colonel Lágrimas*

'Paulina Flores deftly captures our startling humanity; there's awe and dread in these pages—but there's joy, too, fleeting and overwhelming. The worlds she crafts in *Humiliation* are our worlds, in all their terror and amazement.'

Bryan Washington, author of *Lot*

'An incredible storyteller. Paulina Flores has a knack for laying bare those fragile, often unarticulated, often hard to pin down emotions children hold for their parents.'

Jennifer Nansubuga Makumbi, author of *Kintu*

Contents

Humiliation

Are we almost there?" moaned Pía. "I'm tired."

Simona watched her younger sister panting and dragging her feet. "Shhhh," she said, "quit whining."

They had been walking for over an hour on the side of the street where the sun beat down hardest. Their father was a few steps ahead. He had realized too late that the shade was on the other side, and the cars speeding down Bellavista wouldn't let them cross now. In any case, the uneven number they were looking for was on this side, the sunny one, and they were nearly at their destination.

"Dad! I'm tired!" said Pía, and she sat down on the hot ground with her legs outstretched.

Simona watched her father. He didn't seem to hear Pía and went on walking.

"Dad!" Pía shouted.

This time he turned around, came back, and picked her up. As he went on walking resignedly, Pía's head peeked over her father's shoulder like a puppet taking the stage. She hugged his neck tightly and smiled in victory.

Simona raised her eyebrows and shot her sister an angry look, letting her know just how much work she gave other people by being so little. Still, she couldn't help feeling a little bitter.

Simona was tired too, but she was too big for her father to carry her.

The year was 1996. The girls were nine and six years old. Their father was twenty-nine, and unemployed.

Simona had to hurry to catch up. Her father's strides grew even longer and faster. His jaw was clenched as he walked, or at least it looked that way from what she could see of him. He was nervous, thought Simona. But seeing him tense today didn't make her sad like other times; instead, her chest filled with pride. It meant that her father cared about what was happening. And what was happening, what was about to happen, was her idea. She put her hand in the pocket of her dress and squeezed the ad and the map as if they were winning lottery tickets.

Her pride also stemmed from the satisfaction of knowing that she did understand what her father was feeling, and that her little sister didn't. Simona was the one who had spent all those nights with her ear pressed to the wall, listening to her parents fight. And the next morning she would get out of bed to look up in the dictionary all the words they had said to each other that were new to her. Sometimes she even looked up ones she had heard before, but that in her opinion didn't apply to her father: *loser, coward, selfish*.

Simona suffered, but at the same time she loved feeling part of the solemnity of adult conflicts. This was the kind of responsibility that came with the position of older sister.

Since summer vacation started, every morning was a long, grueling walk. Downtown, Providencia, Las Condes. All pretty places, clean and modern. Far away from the neighborhood where they lived. The father had lost his job a while ago, but with the girls home on summer vacation, he had no choice now but to take them with him when he went to drop off résumés or attend interviews. Their mother said they couldn't be left alone. She used the word *abandon*: "You can't abandon them in the house."

At first the father had found it a nuisance. He saw it as his wife taking revenge on him—after all, she could have made more of an effort to find some old neighbor lady with time on her hands who could take care of the girls. Then he decided it wasn't really such a bad idea. Maybe they would give him an advantage. If people saw him come in with two little girls in tow, maybe they'd take pity on him and give him the job.

"Remember, think about something sad," he'd say to his daughters before they entered the office buildings.

"Like if Mom and you died?" asked Pía, confused, the first time her father said it. Her eyes grew watery and intense.

The father corrected himself. "No, no. Not that. Not *so* sad. What I mean is that you can't go around laughing or playing or cracking jokes while you wait for me. I want you to pretend to be sad. Fake sad, like the actresses on TV ... and then I'll take you out for french fries and the three of us will laugh by ourselves."

Pía smiled in relief, happy at the idea of french fries. But her eyes filled up with tears again when Simona told her: "You know what I think about to get sad? I imagine Mom and Dad are going to break up."

Simona raised her eyes to look defiantly at the sun. She'd been warned so often not to do that, but now she felt utterly confident, capable of absorbing all the sun's rays. Because this morning would be different. This morning they would triumph, and all the effort and failure that had come before would be worth it. And she had planned it all. Finally, her help would do some good.

She'd been trying to contribute for a long time. In the afternoons, she sat at the kitchen table next to her father with her own pile of newspapers in front of her, and she went through them looking for any and all job advertisements. She marked them with a fluorescent highlighter, cut them out carefully, and glued them onto a white page. Once the page was covered in pasted ads, she filed it in a folder labeled CLASSIFIED ADS FOR DAD. At the end of the day, she handed the folder to him with all the gravity the situation called for.

She was driven and enthusiastic, but not because she wanted her father to find a job. Nor because she wanted to end her parents' fights, or the family's economic straits. Rather, she longed for her father to be again the way he used to be.

At first, when she found out he'd been fired, she couldn't help but feel satisfied. She didn't tell a soul, but she was pleased. Finally, she would have fun with her father all day long! Every day! And it was summer vacation, too—it was like a dream. Nothing would get in the way of their games: not work, which left him so tired at night; not her mother, either.

Because her mother seemed like the biggest obstacle. She never let Simona spend time with her father: she took over and dominated every aspect of her life, and her little sister's life. She made them food, brought them to school, to birthday parties, took them shopping for clothes. When her father came home from work, her mother went on taking charge of everything herself: checking the girls' homework and their backpacks, drying their hair after their baths, making sure they brushed their teeth well, tucking them in and turning out the light. Simona received a "good night" from her father only when he got up to lock the doors. And then there were Sundays. The day she and her father could finally have fun, her mother would butt in with her scolding. "Don't bother her, Alejandro," she said when he lunged at Simona to start a tickle war. "She's a little girl!" The same thing at lunch, when her father started in with the jokes: "Hey, look over there!" he'd say, and then steal food from her plate. "Let them eat in peace," her mother said. But Simona didn't want him to leave her alone, she didn't want her mother to defend her. She knew they were games, and she liked them. But her mother didn't understand, and she complained to her girlfriends that it was "like having three kids instead of two," or that "he always makes me into the bad guy."

But as it turned out, things only got worse after he lost his job. And then Simona realized that there was an even bigger wall that separated her from her father.

The first day he was home, she got up very early, eager to snuggle up with him in bed. She ran to his room, but when she turned the knob she found it was locked. She knocked a few times, gently, but the door stayed closed until lunchtime. When her father finally appeared he was in a bad mood, and he complained that her mother hadn't left anything to eat. After making some gluey noodles with half-cooked hot dogs, he told her and Pía that, starting now, they'd have to make the beds and divide up the housework. Then he locked himself in his room again. There were no jokes or tickle wars. Her father came out only to go to the bathroom, his face scruffy and ever less healthy. And everything they did made him mad. Things that had never bothered him before, like when she sang the songs from *The Little Mermaid*, her favorite movie. Before, they'd always sung those songs together, and they'd recited the dialogue from memory. "Poor Unfortunate Souls" was her favorite, and the one they sang the best.

"Here's the deal," her father would say, imitating the malevolent voice of Ursula the witch. "I'll make you a potion that will turn you into a human for three days. Got that? Three days. Before the sun sets on the third day, you've got to get dear old Princey to fall in love with you. That is, he's got to kiss you. Not just any kiss—the kiss of true love!" Her father just loved that last line, and so did she.

"If I become human," Simona would reply, playing the innocent and dubious Ariel, "I'll never be with my father or sisters again."

"That's right . . . but . . . you'll have your man. Life's full of tough choices, innit?"

Simona was sure that her father loved her, but she could also tell that something was making him feel lonely, and that all the love she could give him didn't help; quite the opposite, in fact. In some strange and inexplicable way it seemed to weaken him and make him feel more alone. She thought that solitude was related to one of the words her mother had said in their fights, one she'd also looked up in the dictionary: *humiliation.*

So, when she'd seen the casting call a couple of days earlier, it was as if a miracle had come down from heaven. How had she not realized? How had she not thought of it sooner, when it was so obvious? All that time looking at classified ads for carpenters, bakers, assistants, watchmen, salesmen, drivers, and more watchmen, never realizing how bad those ads must make her father feel.

Now, while she walked, she took the clipping from her pocket and read it one more time:

GREAT OPPORTUNITY: Casting Call. Ad agency seeks women and men of all ages for publicity campaign—prestigious international brand. Tryouts: Monday–Wednesday, Bellavista 0550 . . .

Simona loved TV. She always paid special attention to the commercials, because her sister never understood them and asked her to explain.

There were many reasons her father was destined to triumph in the casting, but two in particular stood out. The first and most obvious: people in commercials were much less handsome than her father. To say less handsome, in fact, was an understatement. It's just, her father was beautiful! He looked like Luis Miguel, the most beautiful man on the face of the earth. She told everyone: "My dad is like Luis Miguel's twin." And he knew it too, and he seemed to like it, because he always sang to her "*Será que no me amas,*" imitating Luis Miguel's haughty flirtatiousness as he danced. He turned his face in profile, grabbed his hair, gave a kick and a turn. He moved forward with little jumps, swaying his hips, while Simona did the backup singers' chorus: "*Noche, playa, lluvia, amas.*"

And that was the other reason: her father had a flair for performance. At least, that was what her mother always said: "Alejandro missed his calling. He should have studied acting or something, it's in his nature." Simona caught the mockery behind the comment. And not only because her mother's tone implied it was a joke, and not as serious and tragic as Simona saw it: her father's talents wasted. She knew something about what her mother thought of actors, and it wasn't good. To be extroverted, to draw attention, to show off. After so many reprimands from her mother, Simona had eventually learned that being extroverted was a kind of defect. A flaw that she'd been born with, like the original sin inherited from the first disobedient parents, but without the possibility of redemption. She was a girl who attracted attention and it made her feel small, minuscule. That's why she tried to imitate her little sister, who tended to be quieter and more enigmatic. When Pía wasn't whining she had the gift of seeming simply uninterested, letting herself be loved, never feeling the need to seek out affection. Pía's personality seemed much more appropriate. But it was almost impossible for Simona to be like her; she couldn't help the way she was. And although it had been painful to bear that burden, now, as she walked beside her father, it was something that honored her and filled her with happiness. Because being extroverted was a quality she shared with him. Something that brought them closer, that could destroy any obstacle that came between them.

"We have arrived," said Simona ceremoniously, and she bowed toward the enormous house that stood before them.

"Finally!" said Pía, still in her father's arms.

He set her down with a sigh and asked Simona for the map. He looked it over nervously and then peered at the house, doubtful. It was a big, old three-story mansion, with all the darkness and cold typical of an aging construction, but painted a modern, strident green. A getup that inspired distrust.

Simona saw the hesitation in her father's eyes. It hadn't been easy to convince him about the GREAT OPPORTUNITY. She couldn't let him get cold feet now that they were almost there; she took his hand and tugged on it, saying, "Let's go in, let's go in. They're waiting for us. They're waiting."

"Are you sure it's here? There's not even a sign. What's the production company called?"

"It's just so they won't get so many people bothering them," said Simona quickly. "Can you imagine all the people who would come if they knew the casting calls happened here?" And she pulled harder on her father's hand. "Let's go," she insisted, practically begging.

"Yeah, let's go in, Dad, it's really hot out here," said Pía, not so much excited as imploring a resolution.

"Okay," said their father. "We've come this far, what've we got to lose?"

They rang the bell on the intercom, and there was no *Who is it?* or *Can I help you?* from inside; the door simply opened.

After so many hours in the sun, the darkness inside blinded and disoriented the father for a moment. When he could see better, he realized right away that the inside of the house was also suspicious. Its original structure had clearly been altered. Where the living or

dining room should surely start, there was a wall, a thin partition put
up to create more offices. He felt ill at ease in the gloom of a small
false foyer that allowed a steep staircase as the only possible path. The
floor was of gray stone, the only element that seemed to have resisted
the changes. The worst part was the silence. Too much silence. Not
like a place where people were working. And there he was, cornered,
with his daughters. Halfway between the front door and the staircase,
with no one to receive them or to ask what they wanted.

The father lifted the girls onto the second step and knelt down
in front of them. He took a deep breath, looked up at them. They
both smiled back at him.

He immediately looked away. Poor things, he thought. He
could never meet their eyes; that's why he had to "act the clown," as
his wife said. All this time that he'd been forced to spend with them
lately, it had been overwhelming. They were always *there*, wandering around the house, waiting for him, demanding things from him,
depending on him. Nothing ever seemed to disappoint them, but he
hid in his room because he couldn't even meet their eyes. The truth
is, he didn't know who they were: Who was the better student in
school? Which one didn't like salad? Which one hated taking baths?
Who was afraid of the dark? His wife talked about them in bed,
but he couldn't retain anything. He'd become a father very young.
Too young. Accidentally and without preparation. And he had responded by going along with it. Doing his supposed duty: face up
to it and forget about himself for a time. Leave aside his plans and
projects like a half-eaten apple. Work. He'd spent all his youthful
energy on working, without questioning it much. Leaving a great
unknown between him and what his life could have been if he'd

invested time in his own dreams. Without ever finding out if he could have conquered the world.

It was true that, at first, the most important thing had been financial security. But he also knew that all that time, as his daughters were growing up, he'd been hiding. Limiting his contribution to an exhausting job from Monday to Saturday. And now that he had nothing material to contribute, he felt useless and excluded. His wife was much better than him, and she was right when she threw his lack of resolve in his face. It was logical for her to be tired of taking charge of everything. And all he could do was crack jokes and play games with his daughters. He couldn't think of anything to do but *act* like a playmate, one you casually and miraculously meet in a park but don't know if you'll see again the next day.

"How do I look? Not too formal?" he asked, adjusting his tie. He was wearing the blue suit, white shirt, and brown tie that he always wore to work interviews. He felt suffocated, and he wanted to run away. Every time he had to go into an office he felt the same thing: the urge to flee.

Simona smoothed his eyebrows with a thumb, the way her mother did whenever they were tangled.

"You look so handsome," she blurted, so effusively that she turned red.

"My little monkey," he said, tousling her hair with one hand.

He stood up and started to climb the stairs. At the top, another door awaited them.

"How do *I* look?" asked Pía.

"You don't matter," Simona told her. "Dad's the one who matters."

They rang the second bell. They waited for a few seconds and a man appeared, ushering them in with effusive politeness. Simona watched him with surprised interest. He was a very handsome man, like her father. But his beauty was different. He had dark hair, a sparse beard, and an earring in one ear.

"Casting?" the man asked her father, who replied with an uncertain "Yes."

"Come in, come in," he said, leading them to his desk.

The place itself caught Simona's attention, too. No doors leading to offices, no secretaries. It was just a room in an old house. Enormous and open, with a very high ceiling. Beyond the desk hung a white cloth, and tripods, cameras, and spotlights were set up in front of it. It didn't look anything like the other companies they had visited, but, Simona thought, that must mean something good.

The man settled into an executive chair lined in white leather, and the three of them sat in some plastic chairs that were modern and uncomfortable. He pressed his hands together as if he were about to pray, and began: "Well, then, let me explain how this works . . ."

He told them about the agency, its trajectory and reputation. He said that they operated in partnership with other publicity agencies. That they handled important brands. That now they needed people for a specific campaign, but that they were always looking for new faces. He talked nonstop, eloquently and naturally, about a ton of things Simona didn't entirely understand but pretended to follow, nodding her head just like her father did.

The man paused and smiled. "Now," he went on, and his excited tone switched to a more reserved one. "We need photographs of people so we can show them to the company. They're the ones who give the green light in the end," he said, shrugging his shoulders and showing his palms, as though to say "I am innocent, see ye to it." "The photos," he went on, "are for what's called a portfolio. Everyone in this business needs one, and if a person doesn't have one, we make it for them. The photography session has a cost, obviously, which is fifteen thousand pesos. You can also have it done at another studio." He paused and raised his hands. "Of course, our prices, considering that in general we end up working with the people we photograph, are much more convenient." The man waited for an answer with a smile. "What do you say?" he insisted, when the father didn't answer.

"Good, good, it all sounds good. No problem, let's do that portfolio . . . It's just that really, I'm a little nervous because I've never done anything like this and . . ."

Suddenly a bell sounded. Practically the first noise they'd heard since they'd entered the house.

"Can you give me a second?" asked the man with a smile. He stood up, went to the door, and opened it a crack. A feminine voice—they didn't turn to look—murmured something that the man replied to, also in an undertone. Then he closed the door.

"Sure, sure," he said as he went back to his desk. "It's the first time. I can tell. But you don't have to worry, your daughters are lovely. The brands are going to love them. They have . . . they have just the look we need."

"My daughters?" asked the father.

"Sure. It can't be the first time you've heard that."

Simona turned her head toward her father and bit her tongue.

She saw him sink a few inches into the chair, his face red and his mouth agape. She saw him narrow his eyes as if to focus them better. He was just as surprised as she was, bitterly surprised, and Simona felt her heart shrinking, and the big room around them also began to shrink. Like those torture chambers in Indiana Jones movies, where walls with knives close in menacingly, trapping the protagonists.

"Lovely. Just charming. Look at the smile on this little one here," said the man, turning to Pía, who was grinning saucily at all the compliments. "I bet she gets her looks from her mother."

"My daughters," the father repeated to himself, almost in a whisper.

"Yes, your daughters," said the man, confused. "Well, wherever those genes come from, they're marvelous," he added.

"Yes, my daughters," the father said again, now trying to hide his surprise. "They're lovely," he added in a quietly affectionate voice.

"Well, then . . . who should we start with? The little one looks like she wants to go first."

"Yes. Whatever you say. With her . . . but . . . you know . . ." He paused and forced a smile. "The thing is, I don't have any cash on me just now, I'd have to go take some out. I'm going to run to the ATM and we'll come back to take the photos."

"If you want, you can leave the girls here. You can go to the ATM while we do the shoot."

"No, I can't leave them alone, you know . . . their mother . . . she'd kill me." He apologized and let out an awkward giggle. "But we'll be right back."

The man sighed and twisted his mouth to one side. "I

understand," he said, but his eyes betrayed what he was thinking: "Once again, they're wasting my time." He stood up, and the father and Simona imitated him immediately. Pía stayed sitting another moment longer, fiddling with her dress, all smiles. The man walked quickly to the door and indicated the way out to the street, which was obvious. He didn't mention that there was an ATM at the gas station on the corner. He knew they weren't coming back.

The door closed and the three of them went down the stairs in silence. Simona chewed her lips. She had a knot in her stomach, her body felt weak, and she thought she might tumble down the steps any second. She didn't have anything to hold on to because there was no railing, and her father was on the wall side. Pressed against the wall. He looked like he was about to fall over, too, but his steps weren't shaky. They were firm, or at least they possessed a weight and violence that could be associated with firmness. His eyes were fixed on the ground, his hands were balled into fists, and his tongue darted over his lips. She could see a little thread of saliva that went from one corner of his mouth to the other. She wanted to say something to him, but she didn't dare. She could feel his anger. Because he wasn't nervous or tense anymore—something in him had come unbound. But it wasn't something good. Not for her. He was furious. She could almost hear her father's heart pounding. Instinctively, she glanced at his leather belt. But she didn't feel afraid, just sad at how old and worn out it looked. She tried to take his hand but he went down faster and faster, she couldn't keep up. No, he wasn't going to look at her or give her his hand. And she couldn't stand it. And the stairs seemed endless.

He reached the ground floor and flung the door open wide, and Simona remembered how he slammed the door when he locked himself in his room, and she ran down the stairs to make it outside. To stay beside him. She couldn't be left *out* again.

On the sidewalk, the sun beat painfully into her eyes; she could barely distinguish her father's shape, silhouetted against the light.

"Do you have a bank card like Mom now?" asked Pía when she joined them outside.

He didn't look up. Started to look for something in his pockets.

"Dad!" Pía shouted suddenly, the way she did when she was nervous, on days when she stood in the window and shouted "Christmas!" or "Birthday!" She could feel the tension too, then, and needed it to end.

"How stupid," blurted the father, and he clutched his head with both hands. "How embarrassing!" he shouted, letting his rage loose. "How humiliating!" he said, and turned his face to Simona. He looked her straight in the eyes, which were reddish brown just like his, and she met his gaze and finally she could see her father's contempt. "What an idiot! How stupid! How humiliating!"

He turned around and started to walk, muttering all the while.

Simona stood paralyzed with her eyes full of tears. Her body was shaking. She thought the world was falling in on her, and that she couldn't bear the weight of it alone. Because she was alone. She'd been wrong. She'd made a terrible mistake. She had humiliated her father, and he would never forgive her. He'd never forgive her. They wouldn't sing songs again, he wouldn't surprise her with tickles. She'd ruined everything, she thought, and just when she felt that all the sadness of the earth was falling on her head, her little sister's round face appeared in front of her. Her eyes were very wide, disconcerted, fearful. And then Simona saw her sister as she never had before, and she felt pity for her, even more pity than she felt for herself. Because she knew that her sister didn't understand what was happening, and she did. There would be no french fries that afternoon. And that was enough, that was everything. She took Pía by the hand, firmly, and together they started back toward home, following their father's footsteps down Bellavista.

Teresa

She was coming out of the library when she saw him. Their paths had crossed a couple of times before. Three, to be exact. More or less under the same circumstances. He was riding an orange bicycle, and a little girl was standing behind him on the pannier rack. The girl couldn't be more than six years old, and she had her arms wrapped around his neck to keep her balance. *Must be his daughter*, she thought. Her eyes met his for a second—both of them at once curious and aloof—and then she went on with what she'd been about to do, which was sit on the steps and light the cigarette she usually smoked on the hour, every hour, to clear her head. The little girl also went about her business, climbing down from the back of the bike. Her shoes raised a little dust when they hit the ground. She was wearing a white dress and she looked dirty and unkempt; after landing like that, it was clear why. The man stood up from the saddle but stayed astride the bike, one Adidas on either side of the frame. He kept one hand on the handlebars and with his free arm he pointed, giving the girl instructions. An invisible line leading into the library.

The library's walls were glass and the entrance to the bathroom was clearly visible. Any adult could see it, she thought between drags on her cigarette, not taking her eyes from the scene. The girl headed off in the direction her father had indicated. That was the only thing to do: the girl could only look at her father, his charming eyes, and do what he told her to do. The child went up the steps and passed a few inches from her; dirty white dress and long, loose, tangled hair, she was unmistakably beautiful. She went hopping by, capricious and flirty, taking each step as if playing.

She turned around and watched the little girl go into the library. She saw her follow the route laid out by her father, because surely he was her father—although what kind of father would send a six-year-old girl to the bathroom alone?—and then she focused her attention again on the man, who lowered the kickstand, checked to be sure the bike would stay up by itself, and sat across from her at the other end of the curved steps.

He was wearing a white T-shirt and tight gray jeans. He must have been around thirty. Thin, not very tall. Dark-skinned with light eyes, his hair slicked back, his beard carefully untended. He sat with his legs wide open and he leaned forward, bringing his fists together and curving his back a little. She was wearing a blue dress and her back was also a little curved, as always. Surely men noticed things like that, she thought. She looked him straight in the eyes. He accepted the look and, after a second, glanced away. He was handsome, of course, and he knew it, and he deflected those little glances. And also, she thought, he was a man waiting for his daughter to come back from the bathroom any second.

She kept looking at him, somewhat shameless but also calm. Because it wouldn't go any further than that. She took it as a game, a water-gun duel. She wouldn't invest anything, she'd toss the bottle into the sea without even putting a message inside. She smoked her cigarette in a more affected manner now, as if she were a movie villain. Using thumb and forefinger. During the time it took to burn, he returned her glances a couple of times. Serious, almost offended.

The cigarette took some three minutes to burn down.

She put it out on the cement and kept the butt. She got to her feet carefully so her dress wouldn't blow up, and at that moment she went back to the same quandary as always: Why choose such a short dress? What was she trying to prove? To then respond that it was her right, that they couldn't diminish her own legs, that the dress was a symbol of her independence and freedom as a woman. Her freedom! She threw one last glance at the man. He didn't respond. She turned and walked toward the library door. In the reflection in the glass, she could see him watching her go.

Well, that's that, she thought. The messages, thousands of floating bottles. So common and at the same time always different and exciting. A little adventure, without any risk. Like seeing the ocean through a porthole.

As she went through the door, the man was already part of her past, like the cigarette butt she would now throw out in the bathroom. The bathroom. The little girl. She was so . . . singular. What would become of her?

She thought, as she walked, that if she'd been the little girl whose father sent her to the bathroom alone, she would run away.

She'd give him a little scare. That's what she'd do.

She remembered how once, when she was very little, she'd lost her parents at the supermarket. She'd wandered in the dairy aisle until a guard asked her if she was lost. She nodded. He took her to the information desk and left her in the care of a woman with a ponytail and enormous hair-sprayed bangs, who would finish the operation with an announcement over the intercom.

"Are you looking for your parents?" asked the woman, bringing the microphone to her lips.

For some reason the woman asked for her name, not her parents'.

"What's your name, sweetie?"

She thought for a moment and replied, "Teresa." It was her best friend's name.

The woman with the bangs turned on the microphone, and in a robot voice announced that Teresa had gotten lost and was waiting for her parents at the information desk.

Who doesn't believe a child? Who would doubt a little girl's motives? Do children even have motives?

No, children act without thinking. They let themselves be carried along. They follow the invisible path traced by their father's arm, his charming eyes.

———

So a half hour passed and no one came for her, for Teresa. They sat her on the information counter and lent her some rubber stamps and a blank piece of paper to entertain herself. She stamped thousands of birthdays—hers, her father's, her mother's, her grandmother's, her best friend's. In the end, she signed the document as if it were a will. Because she was always thinking about that, about her will.

Her parents saw her as they were passing by with the cart full of bags.

"Claudia!" they said in unison, surprised to find her so settled in behind the information desk.

The woman with the bangs looked at her openmouthed, and she, Claudia, lowered her eyes.

The misunderstanding was fixed with some uncomfortable laughter and some smiling and head-shaking from her parents. All of them laughing, as if it were a scene from *Home Alone*. No one asked for explanations. No one doubted that they were Claudia's parents, or that she was Claudia and not Teresa.

Children don't lie, but adults are the ones you believe.

The final words are adult.

When she snapped out of the memory, she'd already tossed the cigarette butt and was washing her hands before the mirror.

———

That's what I would do, she said to herself again as she came out of the bathroom, and then she looked around for the little girl.

There she was, standing with a guard, trying to ignore his objections and go out through the library's other door. Lost.

She smiled and went toward her.

"You have to go out through that door over there," she said, and the girl shot her a quick glance and went back to staring at the wrong door.

The guard seemed even more disconcerted at her intervention in the matter. "Why through the other door? Is she with you?"

Neither of them cleared up his confusion. They moved away from him.

"There's your dad, see him?" she said, and then she also traced an invisible line with her arm, like the wake of a torpedo moving through water.

The girl didn't respond or move, just looked up at her with that flirtatious gaze.

"Your dad. There. Your dad?"

He was no more than twenty meters away. Through the window Claudia could clearly see the man who was handsome and knew it. Sitting down. There he was. Even a three-year-old would have known how to get back, but the girl's eyes were empty, as if she were blind.

Claudia turned back toward the guard, uncomfortable. She tried to catch the father's attention with some ridiculous gestures. He wasn't even looking inside. He seemed very entertained with his own fists and the time on his hands. What could she do? The man was already part of her past. She couldn't go back out now, she couldn't turn back the clock. And with the little girl in tow! She took a few steps in the direction her own index finger was pointing, and then the girl took her other hand.

All right. So that's how it'll be.

They walked toward the exit holding hands, and finally the man saw them through the glass.

He opened his eyes wide and jumped to his feet.

She walked with her back even more stooped than usual in her role as superhero, but once they came out into Parque Bustamante she straightened up; she didn't want him thinking she was crazy enough to kidnap his daughter just for one more glance from him. She wasn't coming back for him, but for the little girl.

"Lost again?" the man asked with a trace of humor when they reached him. He had already sat back down.

"She was lost," Claudia said, and she felt stupid for overexplaining, but went on anyway: "She was trying to go out the other door."

He smiled at her. "Thank you."

She smiled back. The little girl let go of her hand, and she was sorry and stood there a few more seconds, dragging out the moment. Would another cigarette do the trick?

"Thank you," he repeated while the girl snuggled up under his arms.

Claudia nodded with her lips clamped shut.

"You want to take a walk?" he asked. It sounded natural.

She looked at the girl, at her head tilted up at the sky, her eyes always fixed on nothing.

"My things are upstairs," Claudia replied.

"Go get them," he said, caressing his daughter's hair. "We'll wait for you." She looked him in the eye and immediately forgot herself, as she'd done so many times before. What time was it? Did she have something to do? Nothing mattered, she would dance in the palm of his hand.

"Sure. I'll be right back."

In the library she put her book and notebook in her backpack, and said goodbye to the musician who always sat next to her at the study table.

"Not feeling inspired?" he asked.

"No," she replied. "I gave it a shot, but it wouldn't come to me." They both laughed, and she felt her face turn red.

When she came out of the library, the man was waiting for her already astride the bike. The girl was standing behind him, her arms around his shoulders, her belly swaying with straightforward delight, like the naturally sensual curvature of any plant stem.

They took a couple of turns around the park. There were adults and young people jogging, others walking their dogs or their children, schoolkids drinking and smoking in the grass, kids playing on playgrounds, older men and women trying out the municipal exercise machines. So much vitality! she thought, with nostalgia or excessive seriousness. She had played some of those roles in the past. She was at the age now when you've already done one thing and another.

The little girl had sat down on the rear rack and rested her head on the seat. He was guiding the bike from one side. Claudia walked beside him without saying a word. She wanted to know more, ask if the girl was his daughter, but she didn't dare. She walked nervously, diminished. She didn't even feel capable of turning her head a little to scan their faces or gestures for the answer to their relationship. It was as if they shone, as if it were dangerous to look directly at them. She also felt as if she were crossing a boundary, that she was finally acting in accord with the messages thrown into the sea. A man had told her once, "You waste the impulse, desire is fleeting." She'd found his phrasing grandiloquent and replied that the problem was that it was never fully satisfied. Desire. But she said it to get him away from her, because she wasn't sure about taking a risk on him. Maybe now she would manage to find out a little more. She began imagining what he would be like, how he would act, and then his voice interrupted her.

"And your name is . . . ?"

"Teresa," she said with a certain coldness. Without looking at him, and resuming the silence.

"And I'm Bruno," he said with a hint of irony, showing her he was aware of all the things she was hiding.

A black dog approached them and started to bark. At her, not at the bicycle wheels, as dogs usually did. As she walked, it barked and followed her at a distance, with hatred, fearlessly.

Dogs bark at ghosts or thieves, she thought. Which was she?

"Why do dogs bark at you, Teresa?"

"They know I'm thinking bad thoughts."

"That's right, I'd forgotten dogs can tell that."

"They've sort of forgotten, too."

"Dogs just ain't what they used to be," he said. And then Claudia could finally look him in the eyes again. They were blue, and they sparkled.

The dog stayed behind with a pack of strays all sniffing one another. It barked one last time.

Claudia took out a cigarette and offered him the open pack.

"I don't smoke in front of her."

"Right."

"You want to have *onces* with us? I live around the corner." His tone was still decisive, but it didn't sound calculated. Not entirely. If he had presumed to have total confidence in his suggestion, she would have left right away.

"Sure," she said, and they began an awkward conversation.

"Where do you live?"

"Not so close."

"Sure. What were you doing at the library?"

"Nothing."

"Sure."

"I was reading."

"Reading what?"

"The civil code." It was what almost everyone read at the library. It sounded realistic.

"Sure," he said again.

They reached the door of an old building. "This part's going to be a little harder," said Bruno. "It's on the fourth floor," he added, hefting the bike with one hand and arching his eyebrows.

What was he doing with a bike, anyway? And if they lived so close, why had they gone to the bathroom at the library and not at their own apartment? Was that the whole point of the outing?

Above them shone the Monarch stockings sign. Neon shins. When she was little and took the bus with her mother, that sign had let her know that she was far from home. Seeing it had filled her heart with something like joy. She couldn't remember at what point she'd grown up and realized that billboard was right in the center of Santiago. So ridiculously and inoffensively close.

The little girl held on to the bike while Bruno dug his keys from a pocket of his snug jeans, then opened the first door. There were two more to get into the building. In each doorway there was a sign that read, "Keep door closed. Crime prevention is every resident's responsibility." *How dramatic*, she thought. *A slogan of the right.*

The floor and stairs were green marble lined with gold metal; they were the best-conserved part of the building. The rest: a dark hallway with dirty walls, suspicious doors, broken glass.

The little girl went up first, wielding the keys, then Bruno with the bike. Claudia followed behind, taking care the back wheel didn't hit her. After climbing the last step she found the door to apartment K open. She waited, indecisive, raising her hand to her mouth and biting a nail. She could still turn around and leave.

"Come on in," he called from inside.

She did what she always did in such situations, which was repeat the advice she'd read in a horoscope when she was fifteen: "Leap into the unknown and have faith." She took the next step.

Bruno's voice called again from the next room: "You can leave your backpack there."

She dropped it where she was standing. It didn't seem to matter, given the apartment's decoration: nonexistent. Except for a collapsible table, some plastic stools, a mirror, and two square wool mattresses on the floor, there was nothing there. No photos or pictures, no ornaments, no waste. It was disconcerting that a guy who seemed so concerned about his appearance would live in an empty house. And it intrigued and astonished her in equal measure. She wondered who he really was, who the two of them were.

The walls were high, with rounded moldings. The only window in the living room looked out onto the building's inner courtyard. It didn't let much light in, and the view consisted of clothes and towels hung out to dry on the balconies of neighbors across the way.

Above the mattresses, some numbers were written on the wall. They looked like a phone number. Scratches on the parquet floor bore witness to furniture that had once been there, and was dragged away.

For a second she thought Bruno would shout from the other room that they'd just moved in. Although in any case that wasn't the answer she was looking for, and it wouldn't explain the apartment's enigmatic precariousness. Despite the lack of personal expression, and the fact that there wasn't a single object that would give a clue about the person or people who inhabited the space, she got the feeling they had lived there for a long time. An intense, warm smell of daily routine seemed to confirm her suspicion—the space seemed intentionally sparse. There was something premeditated about the emptiness, and that—the choice of absence—surprised her all the more. Ultimately, it said as much about him as if the apartment had been full of collectible comic book figurines.

Bruno appeared holding a bowl of Cocoa Puffs floating in milk in one hand, a bottle of red wine and two glasses in the other. He called to the little girl. She came running in from another room, took the bowl, and disappeared again. When Claudia heard a door close she felt the regret return—once again she hadn't been able to observe the girl's face closely, decipher her features. Although now it wasn't the similarity with her father that made her uneasy. She wanted to look for traces of the mother. Because there must be one, she told herself. Somewhere, a woman existed who had that little girl's features. Where?

Bruno offered her one of the mattresses to sit on. He brought a stool over, put the glasses on it, and poured the wine. When she drank at her house she used cups; she knew nothing about wines, and neither the bottle nor the vineyard gave her any clue as to this one's quality. She still wouldn't know after tasting it. He sat down on the other mattress and took one of the glasses, rested his head against the wall, and waited for her to pick the other one up and toast.

"To chance meetings," said Bruno.

They took the first sips in silence. He asked her for a cigarette. She took out two and they smoked, also without speaking. She could hear a woman's voice somewhere saying, "Of course, of course, yes, of course." Her voice was emphatic and she must have been talking on the phone, because there was no reply.

A small, transparent ring appeared on the white wall and slid down over the wooden floor. Claudia knew the circle was inside her eye. She had gone out with a man once who didn't eat sugar and he told her it was very normal, that those shapes appeared when you were deficient in a certain protein. He'd told her the name of the protein, but she didn't remember. In any case, she still attributed the phenomenon to a mixture of anxiety and stillness. She got up and walked over to the window. On the outside ledge she found some shells, the first decoration—or the closest thing to a decoration—she had seen there. She toyed with them awhile, wondering what Bruno was doing. Was he looking at her, at her back, or the hem of her dress and her legs? Was he looking down at his fists again? She didn't want to turn around and find out, and she kept playing with the shells. She felt their rough folds and wished he would come closer, maybe embrace her. But she knew he was not that sort of man, the kind who accompanied you—not to the bathroom or to look out the window.

Suddenly she said, "So . . . that whole deal with the lost little girl . . . Is that how you get women to your apartment?" What a humiliating sentence, another conservative sentiment.

"Sure, that's our strategy," he answered, and he winked at her when she turned around.

Claudia walked back over to him and sat down again on the mattress. She took a long sip of wine, set the glass aside, and rested her hands on her bare knees. She looked toward the wall, and she could tell her posture held an air of defeat. He moved closer and laced his fingers with hers, picked up her hand between his, and they turned to face each other. Claudia was uncertain as she looked at him, but he pressed his forehead against hers and smiled.

He took her by the waist and sat her on his knees, facing him. Claudia caressed his shoulders, the dark skin of his arms, following the slight curve of his muscles. He had a lizard tattooed on his forearm. Just the outline in black, but it didn't seem unfinished. Same as the apartment, it was how it had to be. She traced the line of the drawing with a finger and then tugged on his sparse hairs. They were short and thin, like a child's.

"Hold on to my neck," he said.

She did as he told her, and Bruno got up from the mattress. She wrapped her legs around his waist, rested her head on his chest, and felt his hammering heart, his agitated breathing. She wanted him to bring her quickly to his bed, and that's what happened. Holding on to his body, clutching him, she felt a marvelous vertigo. How entertaining life could be. She was no longer nervous or scared; she was on solid ground. And all because of coincidence, to good luck. To cling like that to a man.

They went to the bedroom. Bruno asked her to push the door closed with her legs, and as she did she remembered the girl. Remembered that they weren't alone. She was still on top of him as he sat on the bed. He looked at her and clicked his tongue on his slightly sunken teeth. She wanted to ask if they had to be quiet, but before she could say anything, he took her by the throat, squeezed slowly, and then moved his hand to her mouth, covering it, and then squeezed her throat again, hard.

This room was even darker than the other one, and it was totally different. It looked like a conventional master bedroom. Wooden bed frame, double bed, bedside tables on either side with matching lamps. Rugs on either side. A plasma TV over a three-drawer dresser. Embossed copper pictures on the wall with images of horses and bulls running. Flowers in the window, metal blinds, sky blue and old. It was all familiar to Claudia, it was as if she belonged there, with this strange family and their strange way of inhabiting places.

———

"I didn't think it would be like this," she whispered, looking at the furniture.

"Oh no?" he replied, and he caressed her head just as he'd done with the little girl a while before. "I'm sure you did."

He started to kiss her neck while he held her hair back, making a ponytail and tugging on it a little, and then he stroked her back, following the line of her spine. In spite of his assurance and the strength with which he'd carried her to bed, his hands were trembling.

"You like that?" he asked as he licked her earlobe.

"Yes."

"It doesn't matter that it's going to end?"

"No."

Bruno lay back on the bed and brought Claudia with him, his hand on the nape of her neck. She kissed him and started to rock back and forth on top of him.

"Do you want to take my clothes off?"

"I'd love to."

He squeezed Claudia's thighs with his hand and went down until he reached her sneakers. He took them off carefully, gently, and did the same with her socks. He caressed her bare feet. He lowered the zipper on her dress and pulled it off over her head, eagerly, and always with a tremor in his hands and breathing, as if as if he were suffering somehow.

She'd always enjoyed being naked on top of a clothed man, and she started to take off her underwear. Before she could get rid of it entirely, he took her by the shoulders and turned her and laid her down on her side in front of him. He pulled down the left cup of her bra with a kind of fury, and he pushed in her nipple with his finger. He pressed and massaged, and she was very close to him, yearning, her mouth open, thirsty and generous. She could smell Bruno's scent, citric. A familiar smell, one she'd smelled on other men, and it made her want to ask him where he worked, how he made a living.

He squeezed her throat hard again, then tenderly caressed her eyebrows. He licked her breasts and felt between her legs to see if she was wet, and when he found that she was, he let out a sigh of pleasure and kept his hand there and he put the fingers of his free hand into her mouth, slowly, waiting for her to lick them, and that's what she did.

Bruno's body tensed and he pushed Claudia's belly with his knee and started to rub against her. The way he touched her and took her acquired a certain violence, but not a dominating one; to her surprise, it was a clumsy, inexpert thrust. She looked at him. He was licking his lips and it seemed like something in him was contracting. He was completely absorbed in himself, his eyes rolling back, half closed in a way that would seem vulgar if another man did it, but not him. She would adore a man like him. She caressed his hair, which was wet by then, and she took off his white shirt, also damp, so she could soak herself in his sweat, because it was something she needed. To absorb the sweat of a man. And she remembered a line from a song that went: "Your sweat is salty / I am why."

"What are you doing here?" he asked. "Are you still sad?"

Claudia took a very deep breath and let out the air slowly. She opened her fingers, dug her nails into Bruno's back, rose up.

"It doesn't matter how many times you come back, Teresa. It doesn't matter that you're sad, because I'm sad too. We're all sad . . ."

And then she started to laugh.

Her laughter, quiet at first, then louder. "It's too late to talk about this."

He silenced her with a kiss.

It was nighttime when she woke up. Bruno lay beside her, asleep. She felt a bit dizzy, but she knew perfectly well where she was and what she'd done. She moved closer to him and breathed in his scent one last time. "My love," she wanted to whisper into his ear. But she didn't. Because it wasn't true, he wasn't her love. Nothing that had happened between them had the slightest importance now. This wasn't her life and it never would be. She got up carefully so as not to wake him. She gathered her clothes from the bed and floor, silent and agile the way a cat goes about its business. She zipped up her dress and went over to the window. Outside, she saw the window of another building, and a red light filtered through its curtains, bright and demonic. She looked at her reflection in the glass. She had circles under her eyes and her skin was shiny. Her hair a mess. What a strange face, she said to herself. Was it the face of a thief or a ghost?

A faint smile appeared.

She left the room, moving quickly, feeling like she couldn't catch her breath. She opened the door of the next room with determination, like a person making an entrance. The little girl was sitting on the carpet watching cartoons on TV. The glow from the set backlit her silhouette. Claudia looked closely at a drawing on the wall. It looked like a vampire, a vampire in the shape of a bird. She felt terror at the sight of that image, but then she looked at the girl, and the girl looked at her, and her eyes, like the girl's, clouded over. Claudia went over to her, ran her hands through the girl's hair, then separated it into two ponytails, one on either side of her neck, and secured them with hairbands. She smoothed the girl's dress and tied the laces of her sneakers. Then she took the little girl's hand, and together, in a matter of seconds, they were out the apartment door.

Talcahuano

We lived in one of the poorest areas of one of the ugliest cities in the country: the Santa Julia neighborhood in Talcahuano. A port town that no one liked: gloomy skies, factory soot that turned everything gray, and air that famously stank of fish. But it didn't bother us to live in a place people considered ugly; I, at least, felt strangely proud of it. We all—Pancho, Camilo, and Marquito Carrasco, and I—felt strong and satisfied. We enjoyed those days, sitting on the Carrasco brothers' front stoop and looking out at the shacks that spilled down the hillside toward the sea, making plans and eating watermelon. That was how we spent the whole summer of 1997. We ate watermelon every day. Pancho and Marquito got a bunch of them from a trucker they'd hitched a ride from in Concepción. The trucker said it had been a long time since he'd laughed so hard, and he let them keep as many watermelons as they wanted. That afternoon, between the four of us, we carried fourteen of them to the Carrascos' house. And when we finished, we sat at the foot of the steps putting half moons of rind over our faces to flash brazen grins at the ruinous place we called home.

I can see us clearly, our happiness on display in our pulpy watermelon smiles. Laughing in the faces of our neighbors, so tired and distraught. Especially that year, when the fishing industry was in crisis and no one had jobs, and unemployed people would wander the streets with servile and defeated expressions, as if they belonged to a vanquished battalion of soldiers.

But my father was the only real military man among them. After fifteen years at the marina, they'd laid him off. But even though it happened at the worst possible moment, it wasn't the crisis that kept him from finding another job. In a way, it was his own decision. He didn't want to start over.

Before summer break started, my parents had a sort of fight. I say *sort of* because, as was usual between them, there was no direct argument, or even—in this case—an exchange of words. This is another clear memory. The family—my parents, my two sisters, and me—sitting around the kitchen table. A bowl of hard bread in the middle, and a mug of watery tea for each of us. Food had been scarce in our house for days. My mother tells us she'd toasted the bread to soften it a little. No one responds. The bread had burned, and now, in addition to being stale, it's black as coal. We drink our tea in silence. Suddenly, my mother stands up, grabs one of the rolls, and throws it against the wall, screaming. I see the rage in the movement of her arm, as if she were throwing a rock instead of hard bread. And when it hits the floor, it does sound like a rock. My sisters and I stare at the bread on the floor. My mother sits back down like nothing happened, but when she picks up her mug her hands are shaking. As soon as she takes a sip she stands up again, this time to go to her room. We can hear her sobbing. My sisters follow right behind her; they sit beside her on the bed—I can see them from where I'm sitting—and hug her.

My father, who has kept his eyes on his tea throughout the scene, keeps drinking it without a word. And I just sit there in the kitchen with him and drink mine, too. I stay with my father and not with my mother and sisters, but not because I'm taking his side. I'm not on anyone's side. Back then I participated in family problems as if I were watching a movie. One whose unfortunate story couldn't affect me beyond the seconds I spent looking at it, and that I could easily leave behind. I wasn't worried by my father's silence, or his empty face as he gazed at his tea. I was happy to remain on the sidelines. I was sure I could get along just fine on my own, with my friends.

That's why I spent almost all day at the Carrascos' house, where Camilo and Pancho lived. We had the place to ourselves. Their father was a miner in the north—the only dad of our group who had a job—and their mother spent the whole day at the Carrascos' grandmother's house with her newborn daughter. Pancho was the younger brother, and my best friend. His barely there neck, broad back, and short legs gave him a rigid look that didn't correspond in the slightest with the torrent of energy he gave off. Ever since he was little, he'd had a talent for concocting adventures and getting into trouble. Nothing dangerous, just childish mischief.

Pancho and I were both thirteen, but there were seven months between us and I would turn fourteen soon. We lived just a couple blocks apart, and we had spent almost every day of our lives together. The Carrascos' house was on Pichidegua, which means "Little Mouse," and I lived on Malal, "Corral." All the streets in the neighborhood were named in Mapudungun. Years before, Pancho and I and a classmate who was half Mapuche had translated the names of almost all the streets. We harbored the illusion that we were discovering meaningful names for those narrow dirt alleys we lived on—I guess we had the idea that Mapudungun was heroic. In the end they were mostly names of animals common to the region, but we still took a certain pride in our streets, especially if we compared them to the industrial neighborhoods around us, where the streets were numbered.

Talcahuano, "Thundering Sky," was the only name that lived up to our expectations.

Santa Julia was born from a land occupation in Los Cerros de Talcahuano, and almost all of its houses had been built by their owners with wooden planks and metal sheeting. The Carrascos' house was one of the biggest, with a second floor, concrete steps leading up to it, and cement walls enclosing the back patio. My house was very small, because my father had built it on the same plot of land as his mother's house. He'd decided to live in Santa Julia rather than accept one of the houses in the Naval Village, which he had a right to as a marine. It's not that he was ashamed of being in the navy—he, more than anyone, possessed the pride typical of military men—but he said he didn't want his children to get used to that environment. Meaning, I thought, that he didn't want any of us to end up in the navy like him. In addition to our house itself, my father made many of the things inside it, from the furniture to our toys. He liked to work with wood, but he could manage with any kind of trash he found lying around: bottles, aluminum caps, powdered milk cans, spools of thread. He used to say that if he'd had more options, he would have been an engineer. My mother used to try to convince him to start a workshop so he could earn some extra money. But he had always replied, in a serious voice, that he already had a job, and as long as he could feed his family, it was enough.

He already had a job.

Since I was little, I'd been used to people imagining my father's job was something great. The neighbors, my mother's family, my teachers, and my classmates all treated him with the utmost respect. A respect that was born partly of admiration but mostly of fear—I suppose because of the dictatorship—and it imbued his job with an aura of excitement and mystery. Of course, for his family, his work possessed none of that intriguing darkness. We knew exactly what he did.

Sometimes when I was little I'd go with him to the naval base, and he let me play in a warehouse full of torpedoes while he worked. I entertained myself with a simple game that could keep me captivated all morning long: bounce a plastic ball against the head of the torpedoes. That was it. The torpedo warehouse was the closest his job got to anything warlike or dangerous. As far as I knew, he had never even been out to sea. He'd gone into the service in search of opportunity—something to do—and he ended up working at Talcahuano Naval Base. Some nights as a guard, mostly as a waiter—"steward," I think was his official title—in the mess hall. He washed and ironed his navy-blue uniform himself, and he

wore it under his white waiter's apron with all the haughtiness of
an officer.

I never knew why they laid him off. My sisters said it was because of a dumb accident in the mess hall, something about an alter-
cation with a captain. Whatever it was, starting then, the resolute
soldier's gaze that had captivated so many people became blank and
indifferent.

It was the middle of January when Pancho announced his plan to us.
That morning, Marquito and I were sitting at the foot of the steps.
Marquito was the Carrascos' cousin. He was twelve, the youngest
of the group. He lived close by, on Cahuello ("Horse"), and like me
he spent all day at his cousins' house. At first his mother had sent
him there so her sister could watch him while she worked, and then
he became one of us.

While we waited for the Carrasco brothers to wake up, we
were trying to translate the lyrics of the Smiths' song "The Headmaster Ritual" into Spanish.

Before the semester had ended, Pancho and I had stolen
two English dictionaries from school. The idea was to translate
the lyrics of our favorite bands over the summer vacation. Back
then we were hooked on the Smiths. There was a music store in
Conchester—our nickname for Concepción—and we'd spent so
much time there looking and admiring without buying anything,
the sales guy had offered to record whatever albums we wanted;
we only had to bring him blank cassettes. We whiled away whole
afternoons talking to him. He told us that Morrissey had named
his band the Smiths because it was one of the most common and

unrefined last names in England, and he thought it was time to show the vulgar side of the world. Our eyes shone when we heard stories like this. We wanted to be like Morrissey. We felt just as common and just as superior.

Pancho burst through the front door of his house. "I've got it all planned out," he said.

Marquito and I turned and looked up at him. He was tapping his head with his index finger, repeating, "It's all right here." He was just waking up; his hair was tousled and his eyes bloodshot. He sat down beside us and looked straight ahead with that unhinged look he had whenever he was plotting something. Marquito and I put our dictionaries aside and waited for him to tell us what he had in mind, but Pancho said nothing. He just breathed deeply, as if trying to calm his thoughts.

"Where's Camilo?" he asked suddenly.

"Wasn't he with you, sleeping in your room?" I asked, and I picked up the dictionary again. I flipped to *J* to look up the word *jealous*, from "jealous of youth."

"What?" asked Pancho, confused. He jumped up and went back inside.

A gust of air whipped up eddies of dust in the street, and I shielded my eyes. The wind never left Talcahuano, no matter the season. Pancho reemerged, this time with wet hair and some slices of watermelon that he handed out.

He took a couple of bites and then declared: "We're going to steal the church's instruments. I call dibs on the guitar."

"I thought the plan was to translate songs," I said.

"Now we're going to do both," he replied, not looking at me as he spat out some watermelon seeds. Pancho always wanted to do everything at once.

"Which church?" asked Marquito.

"Betsabé's dad's church," replied Pancho. He stood up again. He went into the house and put on "The Headmaster Ritual," the song we were translating. He turned the volume all the way up and started to dance, moving his arms like he was having an epileptic fit, and he took a running leap from inside the house to the street.

Betsabé was the daughter of the pastor of Talcahuano's evangelical ministry, Blessed to Bless. We had played with her when we were little, until her father really embraced religion and became a pastor. That summer, Pancho had a crush on her. The truth was, we were both trying to woo her, but Pancho was more persistent than I was and he went to the pastor's meetings—that's what evangelicals called the kind of masses they held—just so he could see her. He'd gone to a meeting the day before, and that's where he'd had the idea for the heist.

He told us it was like he'd had a mystical enlightenment while everyone was raising their arms to the sky, shouting Hallelujah and chanting, "He lives, He lives. He returned from the dead. He lives, He lives. We will celebrate." That was when he started paying attention to the accompanying music played by a band on a small stage to one side of the pastor's pedestal. According to him, he saw the instruments floating in the air without the musicians who were playing them: guitar, bass, drums, and keyboard. He felt that God was appearing to him and revealing a new mission; basically, God

wanted him to steal the instruments. We had decided the year before that God didn't exist, or that if he did, we weren't interested
in him. But still, it wasn't strange to hear Pancho say such things.
There was something about the evangelicals that just fit with his
personality: the ecstacy, the delerium of fanaticism. You could
imagine him as a Christian who converted after years of sinning, or
as a self-proclaimed prophet who went into mystical trances in the
middle of a small-town plaza, surrounded by a small group of loyal
followers—people like Marquito and me.

When Camilo appeared, Pancho still hadn't managed to entirely explain his new plan. Camilo was a year older than Pancho.
He was short like his brother, but thinner. He didn't seem any
older physically—or in any of his abilities—but he compensated
by being more violent. He was prone to fistfights, especially with
Pancho. He was wearing only the pair of sweatpants that he never
took off, not even to sleep, and he held a slice of breakfast watermelon in his hand. He greeted us with a raise of his eyebrows and
sat on the ground a little away from the three of us. He leaned his
head grumpily against the wall of the house, as though to make
it very clear he wasn't at all interested in whatever Pancho was
plotting.

With Camilo to one side and the three of us at the foot of the
steps, we were finally all assembled. I can see us as the inoffensive gang that we were, each of us playing his role. Marquito the
kid, Camilo the troublemaker, Pancho the impulsive agitator, full
of crazy ideas, and me, the other side of the coin and his faithful sidekick—serene and quiet, thoughtful. We sit there listening
to Pancho, who's so enraptured with his plans, he stumbles over
his own words and can't finish one sentence coherently before

launching into another, just like the surf down below us: before one wave can break, the next is on top of it. Marquito and I interrupt him every once in a while to ask him to get to the point.

The most important thing was that the instruments were stored in the church at night. That's what the bassist had told Pancho when he went up to compliment the band and pump them for information.

At first, Camilo seemed indifferent to Pancho's plan and his intensity. But then he asked, suspiciously: "And how are we going to divide up the instruments? Dibs on the guitar."

That interruption led to a fight between the brothers that lasted, intermittently, until well into the afternoon. They finally agreed that Camilo would play drums, Pancho guitar, Marquito bass, and I would play keys. I liked the idea of playing keyboard. It seemed like an instrument that went with my personality—keyboard players tended to be mild-mannered and intellectual guys. Although, had I been able to choose, I would have gone with the guitar.

By the end of that day we were all as excited as Pancho about the new plan, and we decided to go over the details in the following days. As I was leaving, I saw that someone had written on the curb with a piece of charcoal:

Give up education as a bad mistake.

Walking home, I felt excited as I thought about what the coming days would hold. I didn't know how the whole matter of the heist would turn out, but thinking about it filled me with energy and confidence. Above all the uncertainty and adversity I could see ahead, there prevailed a feeling of invulnerability that lifted me up. I imagined us sneaking into the evangelical church at night and emerging triumphant. The goal of stealing the instruments was diffuse—I couldn't exactly picture myself playing "How Soon Is Now?" on the keyboard. I just saw myself and the Carrascos having a ball with some instruments we would never have been able to pay for.

At home I was hit by the aseptic smell of bleach that had pervaded the house for weeks now. A new smell, and one that contrasted with the familiar scent of damp, burned wood that used to reign. My mother had been obsessed with hygiene and order ever since she'd gotten work cleaning houses for some families in Concepción.

Everything was dark except for my mother's room, where she and my sisters were talking and laughing. She had never worked outside the house before, and I figured they were happy to get to spend some time together the way they used to. They were listening to a cassette of mine, by Los Tres. I heard how they laughed and sang: *Quién es la que viene ahí, tan bonita y tan gentil.* I stayed hidden in the dark behind the half-drawn curtain that served as a door. It was strange to see my mother cheerful. She looked especially young, almost like one more sister. My father wasn't home. I spied on them for a while, and at a certain point my older sister, Carola, looked over to where I was standing. I thought she would call me out and say something mean—for a while now she had been constantly reproaching me, though I didn't know for what—but instead she pretended not to see me. She started singing louder, almost shouting, and she snapped her fingers while she danced, shimmying in a ridiculously provocative way, making my little sister and my mother laugh and clap in encouragement. I stared at Carola, knowing that she knew I was watching, and for a second, watching her from the shadow, I remembered how much fun we'd had when we were little. I remembered how close we'd been back then, when it was just the two of us. I went to the bedroom then and lay faceup on the bed, and I listened to them sing and laugh until very late, when my father got home.

His key turned in the lock, and in a few seconds the house was silent. He walked straight down the hall. I saw his dark profile outlined in the bedroom doorway, his head high. He still had his marine's haircut, shaved at the neck and smoothed to one side at the crown, his cheeks shaved close and his mustache meticulously trimmed, though he had nowhere to go. I could almost catch a whiff of his English cologne from my bed. But it was impossible to relate such a fresh smell to his flaccid face and listless expression. He didn't greet me. Maybe he thought the room was empty or that I was asleep. Maybe he just didn't want to say anything. I didn't greet him, either. He took a deep breath and went into the bathroom. Then he left the house again, and I didn't hear him come back.

The next morning Pancho was waiting for me, sitting on the steps with a pile of books beside him. He looked even more agitated than the day before, and he seemed to have gotten up very early or not slept at all. In an enigmatic tone, he informed me he'd had an amazing idea for the heist, and he'd tell us about it once we were all there. The books he had turned out to be encyclopedias and dictionaries, stolen from who knows where. Marquito arrived soon after with the bag of tobacco; he sat on the steps and started right away to roll a cigarette. Marquito had an innate talent for rolling. We collected the tobacco from cigarette butts we picked up in the street and stashed in newspaper. Marquito also took care of the rolling papers—he stole them from his mother's purse.

Pancho took the cigarette Marquito handed him and took a deep drag, then said: "This is the last smoke." He showed it to each of us, then brought it close to his face and looked at it as though saying a last goodbye, and he flicked it away with his thumb and index finger. "We're going to have to make some sacrifices to get the goods."

"And you're going to make us?" Camilo suddenly appeared in the doorway. Pancho replied with a sigh and a condescending smile.

"I never said this was going to be easy. But if you'll just let me explain." Pancho paused and filled his lungs with air. "We're going to give up smokes because we're going to start training for the robbery." He stood up again and looked at us with his eyes wide, excited. "Because we're going to train in the ancient Japanese art of espionage and guerrilla war: *ninjutsu*."

"Ninjas?" said Camilo, laughing uproariously. "You want us to dress up like ninjas? Like the Ninja Turtles?"

Pancho's eager smile vanished for an instant.

"Let me finish, Camilo," he said, annoyed, but he didn't explain any further. He was quiet for a moment and then he turned to me. "What do you think?" His eyes begged for approval.

"Yeah, what does our little brain think?" said Camilo.

"I don't know . . . aren't ninjas supposed to be the bad guys in movies?" I asked doubtfully. Pancho's eyes lit up and his confident smile returned.

"And how are we supposed to just turn into ninjas from one day to the next?" asked Camilo, which led to another fight between the two brothers. Marquito and I took the chance to roll and smoke the cigarette Pancho had robbed us of.

Pancho had a talent for mixing things together and complicating them. He came up with one idea after another and didn't follow through on any, although that didn't take away from the marvelously authentic way he invented his schemes, fascinating in its unreflective spontaneity. It was as if, for Pancho, the world were a place specially designed to astonish him in particular. Even today I can picture him absorbed in thought, his face determined. I suppose Camilo envied him, and that's why he used to make fun of him. Next to Pancho, everyone else seemed like a fraud.

Camilo sank his fist into Pancho's ribs and said: "Okay, okay, what's the plan?"

Pancho explained that there really wasn't much information about *ninjutsu*, so for now we would read what he'd found in some encyclopedias, and then we'd see what we should do next.

"And why don't we try something else?" asked Marquito. "I took some kung fu classes at school." Pancho raised his hands to the sky, as if to say "Finally."

"We're going to learn the art of *ninjutsu* because ninjas are like us." His tone was so ridiculously solemn that even he couldn't help but burst out laughing. Then he calmed down, hopping in place a couple of times, and looked at us with a seriousness that was comical for being forced. He nodded, as if agreeing or convincing himself of something, and then he couldn't hold back any longer and burst out laughing again.

————

After reading what Pancho assigned me—some encyclopedias styled as newspaper facsimiles—I thought I understood what he meant when he said ninjas were "like us."

Much of the information we managed to collect didn't refer directly to ninjas, but rather used them as an excuse to talk about samurais; ninjas were reduced to foils, the samurais' historical enemies. But as far as I understood, *ninjutsu* techniques and combat strategies had basically evolved from those of samurai warriors, and the main difference lay in the ideals that inspired them. The samurais were a military elite that governed Japan for hundreds of years, and their philosophy was full of values associated with superiority, honor, obligation, and loyalty. Ninjas, on the other hand, were mercenaries who always perpetrated their sabotage and espionage anonymously. Ultimately, all the differences that led them to take opposite paths in the art of war seemed to come down to this: to be a samurai you had to come from a certain caste; that is, you had to have a name and money. The only condition for becoming a ninja was that you had nothing to lose. They were poor, so they accepted all kinds of jobs, honorable or not. I supposed that was why they had so enchanted Pancho. And he was right, ninjas *were* more like us.

That night, as I was in bed reading about one of the ninjas' classic modes of operation—infiltrate castles in disguise, hide until the moment is right, kill the guards and set the towers on fire, and then escape—I had a short conversation with Andrea, my little sister. For all I knew, she'd been watching me for hours from the bed next to mine, but I was engrossed in the encyclopedias. The three of us slept in the same room, a small bedroom that barely fit the bunk beds and a twin that my father had built. My sisters took the bunk beds, Carola above and Andrea below. I had the privilege of a construction one hundred percent my own.

"Day after tomorrow we're going to Grandma's," said Andrea as I was underlining the phrase "flee furtively in anonymity."

My maternal grandmother lived in Tirúa, Arauco, some four hours from Talcahuano. We used to spend vacations at her house in the country. My grandmother and my uncles grew wheat and oats, and their land was bordered by planted forest. When I was younger I liked to wander through the eucalyptus plantations with my mother and sisters. We always ended up losing our way among the thousands of stalks, all identical and planted the same distance apart. Of course, just then I wasn't thinking about those days in the country; I barely heard what my little sister said.

"Shut up, Andrea!" shouted Carola from the upper bunk. "You're such a bigmouth!"

"What?" I asked, never taking my eyes from the encyclopedia.

"Stop talking and turn out the light!" Carola protested again.

"Just wait a little!" I shouted. Her attitude with me recently had been exasperating.

Andrea spoke now in a quieter voice: "I said, day after tomorrow we're going to Grandma's house."

"Oh, that's nice," I said. "Say hi to everyone for me."

"You're gonna stay with Dad," she said, speaking even more quietly, a little hesitant, as if she was unsure whether what she was saying was a statement or a question.

"Andrea!" my older sister scolded her again.

"I guess," I said, ignoring Carola's interruption.

I put the encyclopedia on the floor and turned out the light. As I got used to the darkness I could see that Andrea was still in the same position as before, lying on her side and looking at me. I could see her eyes shining brightly, and they reminded me of that classic image of little animals hidden in the shadowy forest in animated movies. I smiled at her, thinking she could see me, but if she made a gesture in reply I couldn't see it. I turned over, closed my eyes, and started thinking about ninjas again.

"Your dad was military," Camilo said. "Doesn't he have a gun or something we could use?"

"I don't know," I replied, uncomfortable. It was true, I didn't know. I remembered how when I was little I used to play with bullets that didn't have any gunpowder, but I'd never seen a gun.

"When've you ever seen a ninja with a gun?" Pancho asked his brother. "We're going to use traditional weapons: ropes, chains, a lot of *shuriken*."

Shuriken were ninja stars. I told Pancho I knew how to make them. My father had taught me to do something similar with a plastic bottle cap and five nails. We used to spend entire afternoons together, throwing them at tree trunks.

We were walking to the plaza to start our "training" when my mom arrived with my sisters. Each of them was carrying an enormous bag. "You guys moving?" joked Pancho. My mother greeted him affectionately and teased him, asking what he was plotting this time. Again, I noticed she looked very young. Her black hair was loose. She greeted each of us with a kiss on the cheek, gave me a long hug, and said they were going to my grandma Clara's. My little sister hung from my neck and told me she would miss me a lot, but Carola grabbed her from behind and pulled her away. "I want to say goodbye too" was her excuse, but she barely brushed my cheek with a quick kiss. She gave Camilo a few little pats on the cheek—he'd always had a crush on her—and she told my mom and sister to hurry up, they were running late.

We used Plaza San Francisco in Santa Julia for training. It was ideal because it had a playground built of metal and wood where we could exercise without anyone bothering us, since the equipment was so old and shabby that almost no kids ever used it. In the end we couldn't find much more information about *ninjutsu*; so just like that, with a little knowledge and no *sensei*, we trained in the things our intuition told us were essential. Supposedly, *ninjutsu* meant "the art of stealth," so we focused especially on learning how to slip away, how to make all our movements silent.

We practiced our balance on the teeter-totter and climbed whatever was in front of us, from the playground equipment to the walls guarding houses or abandoned factories. Sometimes we used ropes, but most of the time we climbed using just our hands. To improve our speed we ran downhill, jumping any obstacle we came upon. The climbing, running, and jumping, though—those were the easy parts. We ended up covered in scrapes and bruises, but we were overflowing with energy, especially Pancho, who jumped higher than anyone in spite of his short legs.

What was really hard for us was learning to move without making noise. Ninjas were so silent that some castles had floors that were specially designed to squeak at the slightest contact. They were called "nightingale floors," because the alarm they sounded was similar to that bird's cry. We split up the day to work on the two skills: in the morning we ran all over, and in the afternoon, once our bodies were more tired and less anxious, we set ourselves to quieting our footsteps.

We cleared out the Carrascos' bedroom—they slept in the living room during that whole period—to train on the wooden floor. We left our socks on so the cotton would muffle the noise, and we got into a single-file formation: whoever went first gave the orders and moved around the room with full freedom to make noise. The rest had to imitate his movements, but without making the floorboards creak. Like in a game of Simon Says, except we were raising our legs and walking carefully on tiptoe. The first one to make noise lost. Another exercise: we crouched down without leaning on anything, and competed to see who could stay in that position the longest. I almost always won, and Pancho was the first to give up. Last exercise: we blindfolded one person and put him in the middle of the room. He had to catch us while we moved around him, not breathing, in a kind of blindman's buff. By nightfall we were exhausted, though we always had more energy for the next day's work.

Some nights, or in free time when we weren't training, I searched among my father's things for a gun. I don't know why, but I wanted to know if he had one or not. I went through his drawers, his clothes, some old suitcases, his toolboxes, even my mother's things.

All I found were pieces of wood, and that was strange for him. He had always been so orderly and meticulous, thanks to his military training. Eventually I realized there were bits of wood scattered all over the house. Different sizes and types, almost all useless: broken, old, or burned. I thought he must have been planning to make something, or maybe he was getting materials together to start the workshop my mother was always insisting he open.

As the days passed, he went on accumulating more and more unworkable wood. The house had been a disaster since my mother and sisters left for my grandmother's; the only upside was that the smell of bleach had faded. There were also piles of old newspapers with classified ads circled in marker: "company seeks security guards . . . ," "workers skilled in vibrated concrete . . ." Most of them were for jobs outside Talcahuano, in Santiago or farther north. My mother had bought the newspapers. She'd circled the ads and left them for my father on the table beside his breakfast. She talked about these opportunities in other cities, and how everyone was leaving Talcahuano. Until now, I'd thought my father had just thrown them away. One time he had yelled at my mother that he was never going to leave his house. But here they were now, all those newspapers, like one last chance, though I suppose they held more resignation than hope.

The ever-accumulating garbage in the house was the only sign of life I had from him in those days when I was training for the heist. Neither of us spent much time at home, and I saw him out only once, while I was training in the plaza with the Carrascos. He appeared out of nowhere and started to dig through the trash. He was wearing dirty clothes, his hair was a mess, and he had several days' growth of beard. The Carrascos didn't notice, and I didn't approach him. I don't think he saw me; he seemed really lost. He pulled a couple of boards and a bottle from the dumpster, put them into a bag, and walked off with his eyes fixed on the ground. I watched him go up the street, hunched over and dejected. He disappeared when he turned a corner, and then I remembered how when I was little I had also watched him disappear around the corner by our house when he left at dawn to go to work. I hadn't been more than six years old, but when the alarm clock went off at five in the morning, I'd get up with him and keep him company while he ate breakfast and the rest of the family slept. When he finished, he got up from his chair and I imitated him, then I brought him his military coat and briefcase and followed him to the door. He'd give me a few pats on the head and leave. I would stay in the doorway and watch him walk off in the fog, and I stayed there even after he disappeared from my sight. I didn't want him to go. And sometimes, after a few minutes, I'd see him return, rushed and a little annoyed. His rough hand would take mine, firmly but tenderly, and I would go with him to work.

As for the incredible acrobatics and fighting techniques that ninjas in the movies employed, we decided, after several arguments—especially with Camilo—that we wouldn't spend too much of our training time on them. Not because of how difficult they were, but because we didn't expect to have anyone to use them with, since according to Pancho there were no guards at the church.

After three weeks we'd acquired a certain dexterity, though surely nothing compared with real ninjas. At first glance our training sessions must have seemed poor and unorthodox. But I feel sure that we really did come close to the spirit, the idea that the

fundamental thing was to be practical, to focus on the element that
could save your life.

"TECHNIQUES ARE USELESS, INTUITION IS EVELY-
TING," Pancho would say when he got bored practicing in his room.

"EVELY-TING IS A WEAPON," Camilo would say, kicking.

Those were quotes from Masaaki Hatsumi, a legendary master
ninja we had been able to find a little more information about.

What was an unquestionable fact was that we were prepared
to flee without being caught. We were faster and more agile than
when we'd started out. Still, in case anyone gave chase in cars, we
made some spikes from the nails left over from our *shuriken* that we
could throw down to puncture tires.

The plan was ultimately laid out as follows: we had one hour,
between three and four in the morning, to break into the church
and get the instruments out. Pancho would climb the wall and en-
ter through one of the upper windows (framed by metal that was
so old and rusty it never closed), some three or four meters up.
Pancho's firsthand reconnaissance told us the side door was locked
with a padlock; he would use a bolt cutter to break it. Once that
entrance was breached, the rest of us would come into play: we'd
load up the instruments and get out as quickly and silently as possible. We would escape through the side door that let out onto El
Piñón—a dark hill covered with pine forest, where the route back
would be longer but safer. Once we were in the woods we'd divide
up the booty. The most complicated part of the plan was transport-
ing all the instruments in a single trip without any noise, especially
the drums, which were by nature unwieldy and loud. Pancho and I
sketched out on a piece of paper how we would do it: Camilo would
strap the bass drum to his back with the tom-toms still attached,

like a backpack, and he'd carry it like one; I would carry the snare and the floor tom tied to my back and the cymbals on my chest; Marquito would carry the keyboard on his back; Pancho would carry the bass and the guitar across his body in front and back. Camilo complained that his brother had gotten the easiest part, and Pancho argued that he had already done plenty of work planning the whole thing out. We would cover the instruments with the enormous dresses that the Carrascos' mom used when she was pregnant. If there was time and space, we'd grab some cables and music stands. The amps were a no-go; we'd have to figure out how to get our hands on some smaller ones later.

We all thought it was an impeccable plan. At least like that, sketched out on paper, each of us was a ninja, instruments strapped across our backs instead of *katanas*.

The day of the heist, we felt the weight of the historic, dangerous moment hanging over us. It didn't make sense to train anymore, and plus, just like athletes, we decided it was better for our bodies to be well rested. So what we did was use the morning to wash our sweat suits and lay them in the sun to dry, and then watch the afternoon pass, sitting at the foot of the steps and eating the last of the watermelon. Camilo asked Marquito to get the tobacco so he could smoke a cigarette. He admitted he was just too nervous, and even though Pancho scolded him for his lack of commitment, we all ended up smoking. I told them how that image of ninjas dressed in black was a myth. They used navy blue, because black shone in the darkness. Marquito said that meant our school sweat suits were perfect for this mission.

"Anyway, they're the only thing we have," added Pancho, blowing smoke. We all agreed, laughing.

Last details.

Since neither Marquito nor I have ski masks like the Carrascos', we agree to use black shirts as hoods. The clock in the Carrascos' kitchen says 10:30 p.m., and we've just realized there are a couple of tools we need that their father doesn't have. They aren't essential for the mission, but we can't risk it. I say I think I've seen them in my father's toolbox, and we decide Pancho will go with me to get them; when we return, all of us will go to keep watch at the church. We'll start the operation at 3:00 sharp.

The street is empty, and Pancho doesn't stop talking the whole way to my house. He's more excited then ever. He asks me, over and over, if I understand what we are about to do. "Do you get it? Do you get it?" he repeats, almost shouting. He walks fast, with determination, his eyes staring. But then he looks me straight in the eyes for a second and tells me that we're going to strike big now, and after we do, nothing will stop us, we'll be invincible. I look at him and reply with the same sureness that yes, I do get it, we're really going to do it, it's already practically done. We are invincible.

My house is dark when we arrive, and the first thing we see inside is my father stretched out on the sofa. His position gives the impression that nothing could wake him up. We also see a puddle of vomit on the floor. Pancho makes a gesture like he's drinking from a bottle, and then cocks his head to the side, sticks out his tongue, and rolls his eyes back, imitating my father's drunken face. I tell him to go back to the patio, where the tools are. Once he's gone, I approach my father. I observe his body splayed out on the sofa, my grandmother's old sofa that he had repaired himself using a couple of nails and then stuffed with wool. His face—in contrast to the room, so full of newspapers, wood, and garbage—is empty, expressionless. He looks old, old and useless. Looking down at him lit by the faint light that makes it through the curtains, I think how low he has fallen, and how different I am. And all that time I look at him, and all those thoughts and all that revelatory silence, makes it even more incredible and humiliating that I haven't realized what is happening, and that it's Pancho who, after trying to play a joke on him with the wrenches he'd gone to find, finally shouts that my father isn't breathing.

Days later, Pancho told me that he'd never run so fast, and that in the end all that training hadn't been for nothing. I hadn't even finished shouting for him to go for help when he jumped up and ran out of the house and up the hill. Of course, nothing that had to do with training, with our plan, with ninjas, or with Pancho himself made sense to me any longer.

It wasn't his breathing—or lack thereof—that made me throw myself on my father and shake him, trying to bring him back to himself. It was the smell, the nauseating smell he was giving off. Not exactly of rot, but a strange blend of sterility and fermentation. Pancho had been mistaken, my father *was* breathing. But I didn't have to bring my ear to his nose to realize something was very wrong. It was the stench, the stench that had been emanating from him the whole time I'd been standing there and that I perceived only when Pancho started screaming. The stench led me to stick my trembling fingers into his mouth to make him vomit. I was shaking, my hands and my knees were trembling. My whole body was convulsing in fear as with one hand I tried to make him retch and with the other I hit his stomach so he would spit out more of that bilious liquid that had been waiting for us from the start.

Bleach. My father had swallowed bleach. A liter and a half, a Coca-Cola bottle full of the bleach that a van came by to sell every week. There were cases of people who died from ingesting bleach, although it was almost always children who drank it by accident. Maybe my father thought he would be as susceptible as a child and that he could die that way. Or maybe it was the only thing he had at hand. It turned out he didn't have a gun. No, he didn't think about any of that. He thought only about my mother. He wanted to get her attention. He thought: I'm going to send her a message, I'm going to swallow her job, her stupid aspirations. Her ambition. I'm going to gulp them down and let them kill me with every sip.

Because after I waited hours in the emergency room to see him, the only thing he said was "Call Carmen." After I tried to tell him not to worry, that she was fine, summering at my grandmother's house, he said to me again, more harshly:

"Call your mother."

"Yes, Dad."

"Call her."

"Yes, sir."

And then it was as if I understood everything all at once. I didn't call anyone, and I told the Carrascos' mother and Pancho, who kept me company in the hospital with the others, that I would rather walk home alone.

But I didn't go straight home. I walked along the water in my ninja sweat suit, and while I did, I imagined my mother far away, lost in the eucalyptus forest, and I knew she had left us. My mother was gone. She'd left me alone in the house, abandoned to my fate alongside a moribund man. They all knew it but me. Even my little sister knew and she'd tried to tell me, but I didn't listen.

I reached the port and sat on the stairs to watch some sailors getting ready to embark. Years before, Pancho and I used to come here at dawn to watch the fishing boats set out. We dreamed of being merchant marines. We'd looked at the sailors' faces, stiffened by the cold and laced with wrinkles, troubled and anxious as they went about their tasks before shoving off. We thought we recognized the faces of strong, tough men. Men who weren't afraid of anything. But now, at daybreak and with the black sea behind them, the only thing I could see reflected in those sailors' faces was sadness. A dry sadness that drove into their bones as deeply as the cold on the high seas. My whole life I'd thought that Talcahuano was a tough place, but the truth was, it was just sad. And then I thought of my father in the hospital bed, and I knew why he'd done what he had done. I could finally get a fix on him: my father was a wretched man, but he could still do damage. He could wound, even if it wasn't his intention. I should have known it sooner, but I didn't.

When my mother and my sisters arrived several days later, the house was just as they had left it. I had thrown out the wood and the newspapers and mopped up the vomit. Cleaned the house. That was the first thing I ever did for myself, for me. And maybe I did it in the hopes that my luck would change. Those first days I entered a state of numbness, and I became convinced that I had no choice but to think only of myself. It was as if the garbage my father had collected suddenly struck me as dangerous, as if it had me cornered, as if it could take me down with it and I wouldn't even notice. All the garbage, and the poverty, and the afternoons with the Carrascos— it all suddenly became threatening. Not because of the mission; I wasn't afraid we would start robbing banks. Most likely we would have gone on being a harmless gang, forever sitting at the foot of the stairs, or on some corner once we were older, dreaming up plans that would never come to fruition. Maybe that was precisely what made them threatening. I thought about how stupid I'd been all that time with the Carrascos, playing and bragging about how sly we were, without understanding what was really happening around us. And then the light that made Pancho shine for being so astonishingly him was extinguished, leaving the shadow of a stubborn, foolish, and insignificant boy.

The summer ended quickly, and winter came and brought more wind, plus rain and chimney smoke. I turned fourteen. My mother and sisters came back to the house for a while. My mother explained her version of events to me and promised me things would get better, that we would all start over again together, but I knew it couldn't be like that, and in any case I didn't care. When a person lives through intense experiences, he has the illusion of understanding many things. I thought I understood how life worked.

When I finished cleaning the house I was exhausted, and I thought that I should keep going that way from then on: tire myself out and self-impose obligations in order to get ahead. I thought that would keep me safe. I wasn't going to drift like my father, or fearfully wonder what would become of me. I was going to fight, to sniff out threats on the wind and build a life of my own. Who knows what fate awaited me alongside the Carrascos; I never found out. I left Talcahuano as soon as I could, first to work in the north with the Carrascos' father—my last link to Pancho—and then in Santiago. I got rid of my family and the only friends I had. And I went into debt to study, and I worked twelve hours a day and spent two more riding buses, and I did all the things that people do to achieve a certain well-being, and I got tired, I became a tired person and I lived in Renca, in Recoleta, and in Quilicura, without ever knowing what the names of all those places meant.

Forgetting Freddy

I'm so sad I just might start keeping a diary.

That's what she wrote in a notebook she found in her room. Not on the first page but one in the middle, at random, so as not to give it too much importance, because even with pen in hand she still rebelled against the idea. Starting a diary now, at this point in her life, sounded like a childish and sappy thing. And dangerous, too; it seemed dangerous to write her feelings down. Of course, she'd kept diaries before, lots of them, from fifth grade through her senior year. Every day, religiously, even if she didn't have anything to say. Back then she'd used coded language, aware of the risk the diaries ran, alone and defenseless in her bedside table drawer when her mother did the cleaning. Back then she'd written to someone, as if she were writing a letter; not to the diary or some omniscient voice, but to herself. A letter to the woman she would be in the future. For some reason she didn't want to forget anything that happened to her. She had been sure that when she reached the age she was now, she would go back and read them, and a glint of pride would shine in her eyes, maybe a little smile of complicity. But the diaries were gone; she'd put them in a garbage bag in one of her moves. It didn't make sense to keep lugging them around, they were too heavy.

She started to write soon after returning to her mother's apartment. One Saturday night when not even cigarettes or pills could assuage her. She was in her room in the dark, looking out the window at the sparkling city, listening to the elated cries of people going to or from some party in Bellavista.

One of those people who never stopped partying.
A day for self-pity.

Before, she'd lived with a man. For four years, until the day he'd told her he was leaving. It was nighttime, and they were in bed. Side by side, not touching. Not saying good night. Lying silent in the darkness, hoping sleep would come soon. Suddenly, he told her he had rented an apartment and was moving the next day. For several months he'd been repeating that he wanted to move, and she'd agreed without asking any questions. She didn't act very excited about the idea because she thought that in general, when it came to men, one should never show too much enthusiasm. But she *was* enthusiastic. Maybe in a new apartment they could be happy again. So when she heard that he was moving alone, when she finally understood he was leaving her, she was paralyzed. Not so much because of the fact that he was leaving, but because she'd missed all the signs. Because she'd done what she always did: board herself up in her mind with her hopes and fears and forget about reality.

The man she'd lived with said, "I've been giving it my all to make this work. I focused all my energy on making you love me. I burned all my bridges." And then she went crazy. She hugged herself and started to scream and cry. She went to the kitchen for a knife and slashed the tires of his bicycle. What she wanted was to stab the bed, but for a moment she held out hope that they could still fix things, that it could go on being their bed and she would need it unharmed.

That was the last night they spent in the bed together.

I burned all my bridges, he said, and I was left floating in the water, adrift.

She is floating now, in her mother's bathtub.

She was eating supper with her mother when the attack of nerves came on. They were watching the eight o'clock drama, the story of a businesswoman who falls in love with her driver. "She's too good for him" was her mother's verdict on the love affair, which she found ridiculous but couldn't stop watching.

The butter knife slipped from her fingers. Staring at her trembling hands, out of nowhere she started to cry.

"What's wrong with you?" asked the mother, irritated. It was the same tone her mother had used when she was little and crying for no logical reason. "What's wrong with you?"

A whole life of crying for no reason.
All those times when they told me to eat my food because there were children in Africa who had nothing, I didn't understand.
That's my problem. Never having understood that.

"Withdrawal," said her mother, raising her teacup triumphantly, as if making a toast. Once again, her resentment of her daughter's lifestyle was vindicated; she got up to schedule an appointment with that psychiatrist she'd been recommending for a while now, then went to draw her daughter a bath.

The mother put the inside of her wrist under the running water, like she was testing the temperature of a baby's milk bottle. It was a small bathroom, average, cookie-cutter: bathtub on the left, sink on the right, the lights above the wall mirror, the daughter on the toilet, in the middle.

They looked at each other in silence until the tub was full. Not in the eyes, but at any part of the other's body that would avoid their gazes meeting. The mother turned off the water and tested the temperature one last time. Everything was ready but she still didn't leave the bathroom; she stayed standing there, in the narrow space left to her between the tub and the sink, looking at her daughter on the toilet. And the daughter didn't get up, either, or do anything, not as long as her mother was there. She wasn't about to take off her clothes in front of her mother. She wasn't about to try to take off her shirt with her trembling hands and then let her mother end up helping her. She wasn't about to feel anything, she would be like a vegetable, a head of lettuce waiting for its hydroponic bath. And sure, her mother left food for her every day—not in a Tupperware in the refrigerator, but right in the pot, so the only effort she had to make was striking a match—but no, she still wasn't about to get undressed in front of her. And so both of them stayed there motionless, their heels dug in at that short distance. And then, for a second, their eyes did finally meet. The prodigal son's gaze that they'd shared since she'd returned to her mother's home. The look of a lost sheep. The return of God's grace. But the parable skips over a part, she always thinks. The part when the prodigal son stands up in the middle of the celebration, with his new shoes and his ring, and he listens to the music, looks at the banquet, the sacrificed calf, and realizes he is still unsatisfied, that he's even more lost than before.

To be received with open arms is the worst punishment—the torture of compassion.

"What's wrong?"

The daughter shakes her head.

The mother leaves the bathroom and the daughter locks the door behind her. She starts to take off her clothes. Without looking at herself in the mirror as she used to do. Without spending at least five minutes posing before the mirror to find the angles that made her look better and worse. Without sucking in her stomach, letting it hang out, standing on tiptoe, combing her hair over her breasts, then back, watching her nipples get hard.

Since that day there've been four more baths. The withdrawal set in after the sleeping pills and anxiety drugs ran out. After the friend who gave them to her was fired from the pharmacy.

She'd been taking the pills for three years because she refused to go to therapy. She didn't like doctors of any kind. She found them all greedy and unjustifiably arrogant. Plus, if she was going to be in therapy, it had to be with a therapist who possessed intellectual capacities and analytical abilities superior to her own, and she was sure she wouldn't find one like that, at least not one she could afford. The first and last time she'd been to a therapist she'd felt bored through the whole session. At the end, when the doctor explained the treatment she would have to follow, she raised an eyebrow and was on the verge of blurting out: "Okay, but what was the last book you read?" No, she wouldn't take advice from just anyone.

The mother waits on the other side of the bathroom door, like a nurse in a sanatorium. The daughter remembers reading an article online called "The Ten Most Bizarre Psychiatric Treatments in History," which talked about the baths they used to force hysterical women to sit in for hours—days, even—at the start of the twentieth century. The sepia image of three women up to their necks in bathtubs with metal bars is burned into her mind. Chained up, looking at the camera with empty eyes, plastic shower caps on their heads.

She, too, spends a couple of hours in the tub. She puts her head underwater, blows out all the air, and holds her breath. She opens her eyes under the water and sits waiting for something strange to happen. She expects to see a ghostly figure on the diffuse surface, or a hand reaching in to grab her by the neck. That's what happens in all the horror movies. Something surprising and strange always happens to the heroines while they're taking a bath. She used to think it was a false and stupid scene whose only purpose was to show the actresses naked. Sure, after Freddy has tried to kill you in all your dreams, you go and lock yourself in to take a bath by candlelight. But now she understands the scene's true complexity: it happens that all the protagonists also had mothers, mothers just like hers, who, seeing them so upset, had suggested a bath. "Go on, run a bath and just forget that old murderer."

Today I dried my hair the way my dad used to do it when I was little. He'd plug in an extension cord and then the hair dryer. I'd lie faceup across his double bed with my head hanging over the precipice of the mattress, and he would dry in the direction the hair fell, from top to bottom, as if it were a rug or something. He did it that way because he was practical, not sentimental. My father was a practical man.

She slid down the curve of the tub until the water covered her mouth and eyes. Her nose stuck out of the water, solitary like an island. But she doesn't want to float like an island; she wants to sink like a stone in a river.

As she gets up she puts a hand on the edge of the tub and rests her cheek against the cold ceramic, and then she remembers the brain teaser. She's gone back over this episode in each bath she takes. When she was in third grade, the teacher gave the class a riddle. Whoever solved it would get an A. The riddle went more or less like this: You are in a closed bathroom in a castle, with stone walls and no windows. You draw a bath, but as you do so, the handles break and you can't turn the water off. You try the door but it's locked. If you do nothing, the bathroom will fill up and you'll drown. How can you save yourself? Her seven-year-old heart speeds up and her mind goes into overdrive to find the answer. She looks nervously around at her classmates. She doesn't care about the A, she has enough of them already. What she won't be able to stand is the defeat if someone else gets the answer. She's known how to multiply and divide since first grade, and to read and write since she started school. Her mother prepared her to overachieve, to be the brilliant girl everyone believes she is.

She clutches her seat with both hands, bites her pencil, the end of her braid, her sky-blue smock, and her mind is blocked.

No one in the class manages to solve the riddle, so the teacher reveals the answer: "You pull the plug!"

"It's so easy!" say the students, laughing. But she doesn't laugh; she is mortified. She was unable to solve the riddle. She's been put in her place: she is not as smart as she thinks.

I guess I should have realized then. I see at least three funeral processions go by every day, double or triple on the weekends. When I'm lying down and looking out the window, or sitting on the balcony. At first I couldn't believe it; now it's nothing special. It's not about me, it's the street I live on. I just happen to live along the route to all the cemeteries around here: the General, the Catholic, the Jewish cemeteries, the Parque del Recuerdo and the Metropolitan.

———

Back when the episode with the riddle happened, she'd thought that having a bathroom with a tub was the kind of luxury only millionaires enjoyed. Until she was five, she could fit in the cement laundry sink in the kitchen, and she tried to imitate a solemn pose while she was in there, as solemn as the golden lion's feet on the tubs on TV. Back then her father still hadn't left home and she went to a subsidized school called Pythagoras. Her mother moved her to a different one a couple of years later, for two reasons. The first and most important was that she realized it was a project school that didn't prepare students to leave the projects. And the mother wanted her daughter to be something more, something more than she had been. Something more than something more. The second reason was because Don Osvaldo, the school janitor, was accused of abusing and raping several of the students in kindergarten, first, second, and third grades.

She put her feet up on the faucet to cool down, and she heard the downstairs neighbors shouting. Lately, their voices had been her only contact with the outside world; that, and suppers with her mother. She had closed Facebook and spent all day in a seventh-floor apartment in one of the many towers built on the ruins of old manor houses, buildings whose tenants she held in contempt because they always acted like customers, impatient and rushed. Indifference and forced disdain to emphasize their pride at having made it as far as they had. She didn't say hi either, and she paced, wandering almost all day around the apartment's forty-five square meters. Simultaneously impatient and apathetic, zero dignity.

Since her return she's led a pallid existence, like morning yawns. Half asleep all day, heating up the food that was left for her, eating a little and throwing the rest into a grocery bag she hid in the garbage can. Watching *Seinfeld*, the favorite show of the man she had lived with, but without laughing as much as she used to. Drowsy all day and unable to sleep at night. On these nights of insomnia she still imagines the child she could have had with the man she'd lived with. A beautiful child, truly beautiful, who would have inherited his father's height and his straight, pointed nose. A thought that thrilled and disgusted her at the same time. Because it was what her mother always said about her father, that she'd chosen him for the greater good, to improve the race.

Other nights found her out on the balcony. Listening to the fountain in the plaza that made it sound like it was always raining. Smoking one cigarette after another, her heart shrunken, as she waited for the lights to go out in the buildings around her.

I need to hear something I can trust, like the bark of a dog.

She hadn't managed to be more than her mother. Although that struck her as a consolation, since she never wanted to be that kind of woman. She wanted her life to fill up with dreams, with soft pleasures, to cut off her mother's legacy of rigidity and seriousness.

She had gotten a degree in the humanities and then taken a series of workshops, in search of her true talent. Creative writing, screenwriting, cinema, nonfiction, self-exploration, introductory workshop in organic gardening and seed tray preparation. For a

time, leading that life—a workshop life—had seemed bold and attractive. A brave girl studying for a good-for-nothing degree who
left home at a young age to be with a man she hardly knew. Unpre-
dictable experiences and decisions, the opposite of what her mother
had done with her life and what she wanted for her daughter. That
was what had made the decisions feel brave. The problem was,
she wasn't in college anymore, and she didn't have a man to take a
chance on.

She looked at her bare thighs in the tub. She'd always hated
them, fat like her mother's. But the man she'd lived with had loved
them. At night, before they fell asleep, he embraced her from behind and pulled her pajama pants down to her ankles so he could
caress them. "Special," he said. "What you have here is special."

Once, she'd bought him a Casio watch. She'd bought two, actually,
one for him and one for her. She did it because he was obsessed
with the idea of having a wristwatch, like in the olden days. A metal
watch, expensive, mechanical, that would display a record of its
wear and tear on its glass and hands. A watch that would last forever, that he could pass on to his children, that would be a promise.
She admired him for that. She wanted to be part of that promise
alongside him, so she got him that gift—an inexpensive watch,
but one that at least represented the general idea. So they both had
watches, and one day when they were at his friend's house—all
the friends were his—she said, half joking and half serious, that
the watches were their engagement rings. She and the friend had
laughed, but the man she lived with didn't. In a severe tone, he said
that she'd bought the watch for him out of guilt. That first she'd

bought a watch for herself and then, out of remorse, she'd gone back to the store to get one for him.

It was always the same. She didn't love him enough.

How could he be so sure of what he said? How could he know so much? But that was him, a man who was sure of things, more sure of what she felt than she was herself.

He was tall and solid. Strong, healthy. Standoffish and untrusting with people, bordering on impolite.

"*A man ahead of his time*," he'd said once, reading the cover of a book by Ballard. "That's what they're going to say about me." And she'd nodded, enchanted. She was sure it was true. Because he was smart, the smartest person she knew. And that's why it was good for him to frown all the time, or to be obsessive and severe, to hold categorical opinions. She loved his categorical shoulders, his categorical mouth, his straight, cruel nose.

He was also a man who kissed firmly, like Orson Welles in *The Lady from Shanghai*. And she was the femme fatale who toyed with him. Those were their roles. He called her "the pretty face" to annoy her. She asked him if he cared about looks and he said no, but that they didn't hurt. In the beginning they'd played at that.

Today I found two boxes of dental floss in the drawer of my bedside table. I remember buying them over four years ago, when I'd just left my mother's apartment. I'm sure I thought I would need dental floss, the kind of product an adult should have. The first things I owned were an extension cord and dental floss I bought two for one. I don't know how they've lasted so long—the extension cord got lost or broken—or why I brought them back here in the first place. I can't imagine having them in my hand and putting them into a bag when I was packing, thinking that this time I really would need them.

She sank back into the water so she could hear what the neighbors were yelling—sound is transmitted better by water. Slamming doors and then a masculine voice yelling, "I'm going to kill you." She stayed as long as she could underwater, but she didn't hear anything more. When she surfaced, she wondered if she shouldn't call the concierge to let him know about the fight. Who could say something like that? Then she thought maybe it was okay, that if someone told you their intentions then at least you knew what to expect. Maybe shouting could have saved her and the man she'd lived with. Insults would have made things easier, but they said nothing and then he left.

He didn't ask questions. He looked at her e-mail and her Facebook chats and then he looked at her with hatred, but he didn't say anything. And she knew he read them, but she didn't reply to the absent questions.

"The other day I read Wilhelm Reich," said one friend she still had, "and I realize why you're more hysterical than me."

"Why?" she'd asked, laughing.

"Because your dad was more violent."

And she had said, "Nah, I'm more hysterical than you because I spend more time online."

———

Available, just like the Gmail status, that's how she always presented herself to men. She couldn't help it. She and her friend admitted it to each other. And they shot each other critical glances that deep down hid some hint of fascination. Why did she so like to feel desired? Why did she always have to get the attention of everyone around her at a party? Why did she need all his friends to want her? The hardest question to answer, one she didn't even dare to ask, was why she didn't go all the way and cheat. Was it because she was truly faithful, or because she didn't believe in herself enough to do it? After all, she never went much further than the little glances and temptingly interesting conversations. But he kept watch over all her words, her irrepressible enthusiasm, her smiles, her numerous "likes," the e-mails full of evocative quotations and songs. And later, while they were reading together in their room, he'd look up from his book and shoot her an ironic look, full of rage, and it all tasted like betrayal.

She felt like she fought against herself all the time. Because he didn't allow her to doubt. He cornered her. All or nothing. But she was imperfect, and she couldn't give more than an imperfect love. And in the end he convinced her. What *had* she done first? She couldn't remember. Did she see the Casio watch in the shop window, buy it for herself, and then go back for his? Did she buy his first and then hers? Both at the same time? Had it always been for him, or had she hesitated for a second?

Her mother tried the bathroom door, and went on jiggling the knob a bit violently until she was convinced it was locked. She knocked twice. "Everything okay?" she called from the other side of the door. Her mother was the sort who didn't knock before coming in.

The kind of mother who slept with the door open so she could hear all the sounds in the house, monitor and control every occurrence, because it was hers, her home.

She looked at herself in the fogged mirror and submerged herself again.

She'd loved him, she was sure. She was almost sure.

What else could it have been?

When they'd moved in together and she had nothing, that had really seemed like love to her. Mismatched dishes and silverware, received as gifts or stolen. Two stacked cardboard boxes from the supermarket, a rusty camping stove on top of them, and an old twin mattress where they'd spent the whole day. That was all. Nor did they have curtains, and when it got dark the ceiling was lit by the headlights of the cars outside. And she'd look up and watch as one wave of light after another grew and was extinguished, from one corner to the other in an endless undulation, like the ocean. And that surely had to be love. He was big and she was very small, and a twin mattress was enough for them. Then, when he got on top of her and was inside, she went on watching waves on the ceiling, waves all night long.

And also when it was hot out, when they walked down Monckeberg with the sun beating down on them, burning. He went ahead of her and they walked single file, one behind the other, keeping to the line of shade projected by the walls of the houses. She looked at his enormous shape and it seemed to her that more than sheltering her from the sun he carried the light, he went ahead of her and held the fire that lit the way. While they walked she would try to take his hand, which swung back and forth to the rhythm of his footsteps. And he didn't turn around or notice at all, and she followed him, followed him always, playing until she caught hold of his fingers.

Last night I dreamed I was pregnant and I didn't feel hungry, only thirsty. I was very thirsty, and I drank water and almost didn't eat. My belly was about seven months along and when my water broke, it started to pour from between my legs, a torrent of water, a waterfall. I looked at the pool on the ground, my feet soaked in water, and I knew the baby was dead, that it had always been floating there, drowned inside me. When I woke up I realized it wasn't a dream, that it had really happened; or at least it was similar to the story my mother told me not long after my dad left. "I didn't see him," she said. "They didn't tell you anything, back then they didn't explain a thing."

She looked at her wrinkled fingers. She must have been sitting in the water for a long time. Once, she read an article about some scientists who had finally managed to answer the question of why fingertips get wrinkled in water. It turned out the wrinkling was a trait humans had evolved so it would be easier to collect food in rivers. A useful ability a thousand years ago. For men who definitely didn't take two-hour baths. That question had kept the British scientists at the University of Newcastle so very busy. And she felt like those scientists, and also like she'd fumbled through her whole life that way, with a holdover skill that was useless for her time.

———

She brought both knees to her chest and reached her wrinkled fingers out to the magnet holding the plastic curtain in place. She stuck the magnet to the steel of the tub and unstuck it and she felt relief. Here was an invention that came from useful study.

One of the things that had been hardest for her, on moving from the childhood baths in the sink to the phone-booth showers of adulthood, was dealing with the shower curtain. She was afraid of the inner plastic lining. Billowing in the heat, it would brush against her body in a way that she found perverted. She'd put the shampoo and conditioner bottles at the ends to weigh it down, but they always escaped and the lining would corral her against the white ceramic wall.

After finding out about Don Osvaldo, she stopped believing in Santa Claus and started believing in rapists. No other figure had such a presence in her childhood. Not thieves, not the Virgin Mary, or angels, or the boogeyman, vampires, or elves. The rapist in her imagination was a hunched-over man with long hands and fingers, a long face, bilious yellow skin, shining teeth, and wolflike features. And he would always be lurking around the corner, waiting for her to leave the house to buy bread. But also, like God or the devil, rapists could take on any form; they could be the footsteps she heard at night, lying in bed. Or they could be the shower curtain.

Children had been raped at her school, and back then no one employed the concept of pedophilia, and the result was that she'd gotten things confused in her mind and thought that rapists only went after children under fourteen. Or maybe it was her childish need for hope, for a happy ending, that made her think she'd be safe once she was no longer a child. The thing she was most anxious for when she was little was to stop being little. To make it past thirteen as soon as possible, so she would finally be out of harm's way.

It was a classmate named Daphne who reported Don Osvaldo's abuse. Her friendship with Daphne was based on the fact that she'd been the only one to show up for Daphne's seventh birthday party. As a present she'd brought a set of beads with thread to make bracelets. Daphne's mother was so pleased that someone had shown up, she gave her all the extra party favors and let the two girls dye streaks in their hair with strawberry Yupi juice. The three of them had a very good time, and that afternoon she had envied the relationship between Daphne and her mother. They didn't seem to be missing a father; quite the contrary: they made it clear how superfluous fathers were.

Daphne. After changing schools, she had completely forgotten that name.

She hadn't thought about Daphne again until seventh grade, when her class was studying Greek mythology. The history book had an image of a neoclassical painting that showed a half-naked woman running through the forest with her mouth open, fear in her eyes and her arms reaching up to the sky as they transformed into branches. She didn't turn the page for the whole hour, and she kept looking at it during recess and at home. That was when the image of her friend—the girl with a pink streak in her hair—changed in her mind and became forever that of a nymph running from Apollo. Daphne fleeing Don Osvaldo, turning into a laurel.

————

Her mother bought an alarm to scare off thieves. The daughter had asked, then, if there wasn't one for rapists, too. The mother knelt down, looked into the daughter's eyes, and promised that she would never go through anything like what her classmate had. Because she and Daphne were different, her mother said. She had a father and Daphne didn't. And Don Osvaldo knew it, because he knew her father. Which was true, her father used to borrow tools he needed for repairs on the house from Don Osvaldo. She was safe, because she had a father. And she had to be grateful. That's how her mother ended that speech: "Be grateful." But there must have been something confusing in her mother's tone of voice, in her eyes or her gestures. Because when she said that, it sounded like a reproach, like she was saying exactly the opposite. Until that moment, her father had only to state that the water in the bathroom was the coldest in the house for her to know that he was special, the wisest man on earth. But in the precise moment when her mother revealed to her how fortunate she was, she realized that her father wasn't enough. And also that she was in debt. Indebted to her mother for having given her a father, for staying with him to form a family; it was a debt that would be with her for a long time, one that was impossible to pay off. It would be whispering into her ear every day, forcing her to shoulder her mother's delayed dreams, all her sacrifices and failures.

So she was grateful, but when her father left them she almost felt relieved. She didn't feel all that sad or overwhelmed. Because her mother didn't appear to be, either. Surprised, yes, or that's how it seemed, because of all those mornings she found her awake in bed, her eyes fixed for hours on the wall, as if it were a chalkboard where someone had left a math problem, or a riddle. She thought that what surprised her mother wasn't so much that he didn't love her enough to stay, but that he had the balls to leave. She had always underestimated him.

They went on with their lives alone, more or less the same as before, except that the lightbulbs seemed to burn out faster, the drains to clog more often, and the faucets to drip more frequently. Her father's ghost only appeared then, when they had to press hard on the remote control buttons because now no one remembered to change the batteries. What had surprised the daughter was to find, a couple of months later, her father's drawers filled with stockings and scarves. Or to not have the mirror of her father to see herself in, because they were identical, she and he, the same green eyes, the same long eyelashes, the curly hair, the easy and defensive smile, nothing frank or open about it. Or to hear the serenity in her mother's voice when she told the telephone operators that he wasn't there. And if the caller asked what time he would be back, she clarified in the same calm voice that he wasn't going to come back. Once, even, the phone operator had insisted to the point of asking if he was dead, and her mother, after a second of silence but without swallowing a drop of saliva, let a composed "No" slide out along the phone line.

After a few years they moved to a new apartment, and then she'd left, too.

A drop runs down her cheek, another over her breast. Her body is hot and red. She always liked to take showers with the water boiling. She'd read the labels on the shampoo and stay a while longer under the water. She liked the change that came when she emerged

from the steamy bathroom into her cold bedroom. She liked to feel
dizzy, see fluorescent sparks, and fall onto the bed just before she
fainted. Now, too, she's a bit dizzy, a little out of it. She looks at the
ceiling. It's white, with spots of mold in the corner. When she left,
the apartment was still like new.

Some Sundays she'd gone to visit her mother. They would have
lunch and spend the rest of the afternoon watching *Law & Order*, sitting on the living room sofa. She always fell asleep during the first
episode and woke up with a cramp in her neck. On one of her last
visits, before the man she had lived with left, her mother told her a
story. They were having supper. The TV was on in the background,
nothing in particular. They were both pretending to pay attention.

Her mother told her about the time when she, the daughter,
was two years old and had gotten very sick and gone to the hospital.
She knew something about that episode, but not much.

Her grandmother, her father's mother, had a kind of spiritual
guide named Sister Julia. When they'd discharged the baby, her
grandmother handed her mother an envelope. Sister Julia had sent
it to help the girl recuperate completely. The grandmother spelled
out the instructions to her daughter-in-law, very seriously: every
time she prepared a bottle, she had to pour the envelope's contents
into the milk. She agreed and put it into her purse. When she got
home she took out the envelope and opened it. It was empty. She
called her mother-in-law and asked if there was some mistake. The
mother-in-law was indignant. The envelope contained Sister Julia's
breath; that's what she'd had to mix in with the milk.

"How ridiculous," the daughter said, laughing.

"Yes, I could have just died."

It seemed the afternoon had gotten a few hours ahead of itself and they were left in shadow. They each took a sip of tea, and stopped paying attention to the TV's uniform glow.

"What did you do?" asked the daughter.

"I poured the air into the milk," replied the mother, shrugging her shoulders. "What else could I do?"

It was nearly impossible to imagine her mother young, but she did then. Her mother, who'd always seemed to have such a strong character. More than twenty years ago, this tough and controlling woman had been alone in the kitchen, perhaps a bit confused, pouring nothing into her bottle, expecting the milk to fill up with that nothing. Her mother, obedient, not asking questions, not resigning herself, doing whatever she had to do.

"Your dad told me not to listen to such nonsense, and to throw the envelope into the garbage."

Your father. Her father. Just like the contents of the envelope. Nothing.

They finished supper and looked at each other in silence, with the dusky light and the dry sound of the TV in the background. Everything waning. And then their eyes had met.

"Sometimes, when you look at me, do I remind you of him?"

That's what she'd wanted to ask when she saw the look on her mother's face as she observed her daughter. A sad expression, one she'd never seen on her. So sad. But she was silent, and when they finished eating and the routine of Sunday together was over, she left as always, without a word.

One night, the man she had lived with asked her to tell him a secret. They were lying in the twin bed, still no curtains on the window, the light from outside illuminating the ceiling. The man she loved. He embraced her from behind, brought his lips to her ear, and said, very softly: Tell me a secret.

I was on TV once.

During the investigation into Don Osvaldo's rapes, the school had filled up with journalists. There were lurid articles about the case every day. Features about how he had carried out his crimes: the palm branches he swept the sidewalk with and that the children jumped over as he spun them around, pretending they were the hands of a clock. The workshop where he repaired the students' desks and chairs, and where they found underpants and blood.

One day, at the front door of the school, while she was eating potato chips and playing with friends, some men called her over. Today, she is sure that they chose her because at that age she'd had lighter hair, the closest to blond in the catalog of her class. A color that she lost over time. Your hair got darker, everyone said, as though accusing her.

"Do you want to be on TV?"

They put her in front of the camera and asked her to make a sad face, with her head down, and to repeat "No, no." She would be on the evening news.

The little girl can't believe it—the nine o'clock news! She runs down the street, her heart bursting with joy. The distance to her house seems interminable and she almost can't breathe from the excitement. She bursts into the house, jumping, slamming doors, and hitting walls. She shrieks with happiness. "Mom! Mom! I'm gonna be on TV!" She is so eager that she can barely explain the great event. Her mother looks at her with mouth and eyes open wide. She takes her by the shoulders and starts to shake her. She seems deranged, she's never been like this before. "What have you done?" her mother screams, spraying her with drops of saliva. "Don't you get it? Don't you get it? What have you done?" she repeats, and she covers her face with her hands. "Now everyone will think you were raped, they'll all think it was you." The daughter bursts into tears. The mother gives her one last shake, then turns and paces nervously from one end of the room to the other. "Everyone will see you. They're all going to think it's you."

The report comes on at 9:15, the first story. While they watch, the daughter eats a plate of lentils, because she's very thin and the doctor recommended she eat large meals at night. There she is, spoon in hand, and also there, on the screen. One in front of the other, like twins playing at burning each other's eyes. Because it *is* her. The image is blurry, pixelated, but it's her, undeniably. The scene lasts some ten seconds, and right away the phone starts to ring.

The television keeps you company. TV educates you. Tells you stories. It turns your dreams into reality. I guess I always envied her a little. Her, Daphne. I wanted to turn into a laurel, too. I can't love you so much. I can't love you so much. I can't love you so much.

The water is still warm, but she's ready. She doesn't need shampoo or soap or conditioner, all that's left is to get out.

Then she realizes that there is a scene they never show in the horror movies: the moment when the heroine finishes her bath and gets out of the tub. They only film the protagonist when she jumps in fear or straightens up from underwater, splashing.

She thinks she has learned something about that scene from her most recent baths. When she pulls the plug and the mass of water descends like the floors of a detonated building. When the water starts to flow away from you, to leave you. Because that's what she feels, that the liquid comes from inside her and carries everything away, emptying her. And she wants to disappear with the water, but instead she stays where she is, like a rock in a dry river.

Aunt Nana

I 'm hiding. Enclosed in a vague darkness circled by a floating line of light, the only border of my hideout. Yes, I'm hiding, though I don't really remember why. I know that I'm taking cover, but it's the way a person takes cover from the sun in the shade of a tree. I feel calm, and at the same time it seems I'm waiting for something to quiet down so I can come out. I'm under my bed. I am seven years old, and I hear my mother calling me. She's looking for me. My head is resting on my crossed arms. It smells like dust and the floor is cold. From here I can see the bottom drawer of the dresser and the outline of the bedside table. What stands out most is the rug, the colored fibers that don't quite form any image. But if I looked from the door, what would most call attention in the room would be my bed: its white wooden frame, its flowered comforter. A bed chosen especially for me, like all the things that I have—that I had. But I'm under the bed. Hidden, safe. Maybe I'm playing. When I was a little girl, everything I did was playing.

That intermediary space, marked off by the boards of the bed frame above and the floorboards below, was my favorite place from my earliest memories. My mother's voice gets closer. I see her high heels come into the room. She calls my name one more time and leaves to go on with her search. She hasn't seen me. That's when I come out.

"Where had you gotten to?" she asks while she adjusts my clothes. She looks young. She has bangs and her hair is its natural color, dark. I love her so much. Sometimes, when it's very late and she hasn't come home from work, I imagine that she's dead, that she'll never come home again. I start to cry, and I try to call up her face in my mind. Sometimes I manage, other times I don't. At that age, I thought that the only way to demonstrate how much you loved a person was to see them with your eyes closed, or remember their voice. If my mother didn't come back it would be my fault, God's punishment for my misbehaving. That's how suffering was at that age, visible, exaggerated, for innocuous but concrete reasons. I never would have imagined how our roles would be reversed, or how pain could be a buried feeling that moves silently, building up resentment almost imperceptibly.

"You remember your dad lost his job, right?" she asks me in an ambiguous tone of voice. I nod. "Well . . ." she goes on cautiously, but doesn't add anything. "Go say goodbye to Sonia."

"Why? Where's she going?"

"We're going to donate her clothes. To an old folk's home."

"Am I going?" I ask with a smile.

I run to Sonia's room, and I find her sitting on the bed surrounded by black plastic bags. She doesn't notice me; she's crying.

Her room is another of my favorite places. It's white and looks like a hospital room. The objects that inhabit it are functional: bed, wardrobe, lamp, alarm clock. Sonia has lived with us for three years. From Monday morning to Saturday afternoons, when she goes to her "real home," as she calls it when she's mad at me.

I have two memories that characterize my life with her.

The first one is an everyday memory. We're playing in her room, making shadow puppets with our hands. Nothing spectacular: we bend our wrists and open or close our fists to make swans and snakes that fight each other. I'm fascinated, not so much by the animals as by what we're doing: it's what friends or parents and children always do in movies when they're happy. Sonia's hands are fat, like inflated plastic gloves, so the shapes she makes are always more solid. I laugh, and she tells me my fingers look like noodles; I try to catch hold of her hands, and when she sees the absurd difference in size, she laughs too. Her hands are also very rough, as if she worked in earth and mud, although of course they're marked by the opposite kind of labor, pickled by soap and bleach, the rags and brooms she uses to clean the dust away.

The second isn't a memory of my own. It's a story I star in, but that I intentionally forgot. Still, my parents repeated it so many times that it ended up lodged in my mind anyway. The little girl dials her mother's work number and waits nervously. Sonia, the woman, stays lying on her bed, motionless as a mummy. They stare at each other in silence, and one of them looks at the other in disappointment. They have to wait until nine that night. "Couldn't get away any earlier," I say, repeating my mother's exact words. "She had her handcuffed to the bed. I don't know where she got that idea," I say to myself again, and the voice I use to mimic my mother's is accompanied by laughter.

It was a mischievous act of little importance: there were some handcuffs in the house and I wanted to play with them. It's incredible when something you don't even remember sticks around for so long. Sometimes I wonder why I forgot it. It's not because of my age—I remember things from when I was even smaller. That's why I think maybe it's something more, that maybe somehow I forgot it in order to get rid of a part of myself. As if handcuffing Sonia, beyond the simple game, revealed something; an air of maliciousness, of a spoiled brat, of power.

I sit beside Sonia and she admits that she's not donating her clothes. She's taking them with her, and she's leaving our house. Then my mother comes in and sees us hugging. We close the bags and take them to what will be her new job, a big house where she'll have to take care of an old man.

Since all of that happened, more than twenty years have passed.

This happened at the end of the '90s, when everything seemed to flow or float. We'd rented a house in Recoleta because it was close to my father's job. Of course, calling it "close" was kind of ironic. Before he went to work for the first time, my father tried to tell me about his job: he drew a stick man with an enormous head and a tri-angle as a hat. He drew a half moon as a mouth and two angled lines as eyes. "Like this, see?" he said, pulling at the corners of his own eyes with his index fingers, making them squint. "*Chinitos*. Your dad works with the Chinese," he said, although in reality they were Koreans. He used to repeat it to impress me. But I wasn't surprised so much that people with squinty eyes existed as that there was a whole country full of them. I was struck by the thought that if I went with him on one of his trips, I would be the one with strange eyes. Of course I never did, I never even went to Patronato, where the Koreans he worked with had their stores. Either I didn't under-stand this, or they didn't tell me, but the trouble had a name—"The Asian Crisis"—and it would have implications for my family a year and a half later.

It wasn't the first time my father was unemployed, but it was the most dramatic. He was always inventing businesses that didn't work out, or that he left half finished. I remember that for a time he drove a taxi, and before that he'd rented a storefront on San Diego to sell plastic bowls, cups, peelers, and plates. He said he couldn't have a normal job because he couldn't stand to have the bosses telling him what to do. I guess he was a bit traumatized by his father, my grandfather, who was very strict. He'd been a police-man, and he encouraged my father from the time he was little to follow in his footsteps. The handcuffs had been his. He gave them to us along with a set of batons. They were to protect the family, although the only time they were ever used was when I took Sonia prisoner. Maybe my grandfather gave them to my father to throw it in his face, to show him how unprotected he was, how vulnerable. To remind him what he could have been and was not.

No other project had gotten him as excited as the one with the Koreans. Convinced he was finally going to make it big and become independently wealthy, he took out loans from several banks. An act that my mother was unaware of or hadn't wanted to acknowledge. After everything went under, he would never be the same. He lost his energy, and for a long time he always had an expression of sad surprise on his face. Like a gambler who, almost without realizing it, has lost every last one of his chips.

These are the only things I remember about my father, the things I knew about him and those I was told. Contrary to what one would expect, after he lost his job he spent less time in the house, even less than when he used to travel to Korea. I never knew where he went and it seemed my mom didn't either, because soon enough, the fights started.

My mother was an intelligent and ambitious woman. She was always looking ahead, unconcerned about what she might have been leaving behind. I know because she always told me stories about her poor childhood and how she had overcome it. My mother thought that she could break with her roots quickly and easily, automatically, the way you might shake the dust from your clothes after falling. She was diligent and, for a while, optimistic. She thought it was enough just to be very sure of what you wanted. I suppose that when she met my father, he must have seemed like an entrepreneur. But her plans were always met with an uphill battle. First she got pregnant and had to get married. Then she supported her husband in all of his projects and her husband ended up unemployed, and soon she realized that it, too—her marriage—had failed. Of course, my mother never thought about separating, at least not back then. For one thing, she was too conservative, and for another, accepting failure was to her even worse than the fact of failing itself.

At that time, my parents' story was being woven almost without my realizing it. I was seven years old and the only thing I understood with any clarity was that Sonia was gone, and I had to spend some time alone in the house. Then Aunt Nana came to live with us.

She was my mother's aunt and her name was Monica, but everyone in the family called her Aunt Nana. Though they were guarded by an enormous pair of glasses, her eyes are what I remember most. Black, with no distinction between the pupil and iris, surrounded by some sparse eyelashes that brought to mind a plucked bird. That was her aspect in general, a small animal, shorn and defenseless.

"I don't want you! Go away," I yelled the first morning we were together in the kitchen. She had clearly prepared breakfast with dedication: chopped fruit, chocolate milk. "I don't want you! I want Sonia!" I yelled again, and my voice shook. Nana took a walnut kuchen from the oven, cut a slice, and handed it to me with a smile.

"A person can get used to anything," she said in an apologetic tone, keeping her mouth in a curve, tensing the millions of wrinkles around it. Her white hair was messy, as always. Her skin was dark, leathery, and she had a small hump on her back.

Naturally, I had met Aunt Nana before, but I didn't know any details about her life until later. She was sixty-five years old, although everything indicated she was older, since she could remember the day

she was added to the civil registry. She was the first of three sisters—
half sisters, really. Supposedly she was the daughter of a Turk her
mother had worked for, or so they said. The fact is that she never met
her real father, although to her, that was more anecdote than tragedy.
Also, unlike her sisters, she never married. She was the daughter who
stayed at home to take care of her mother. During the '60s she'd
worked in the Hirmas fabric factory as a seamstress. She handed over
her entire salary to her mother, who likewise decided what was done
in the house and what wasn't. During the dictatorship, the factory
had closed like so many others. She got work as a maid, a "nana," and
after a few years, just after her mother died, she started to take care
of her sisters' children, and later the children of her sisters' children.
It was then that the name Monica was hidden behind her main occupation, and she became Nana, Aunt Nana.

My mother didn't pay her to take care of me, although not because of the economic problems we were going through, or not only
that. The fact that she had nowhere else to go after her mother's
death was as obvious as the fact that in ten more years no one—
neither of the other sisters, none of the nieces—would want her in
their houses. It wasn't necessary to explain the matter further; my
mother offered her lodging and food at least until I could take care
of myself, which would be more than long enough, considering the
years she could have left to live.

I found all this out later, at about the same time I realized that,
in spite of appearances, Nana wasn't as fragile as we all supposed.

"I'm not going to love you ever!"

I left my breakfast untouched that morning. Her dedication,
something about Aunt Nana's friendliness, disturbed me enor-
mously. I ran to my room and hid under the bed. I knew she wasn't

responsible for Sonia leaving. But if not her, then who? To my mind, *someone* had to be held responsible and be punished. Maybe that's what really disconcerted me—I didn't know who was to blame, or if anyone was. I went to school alone, and although I spent the rest of the morning hungry, when I got home I went on refusing to eat. I didn't see Aunt Nana again for the whole afternoon. To disappear under my bed: that was the only thing I wanted.

Not long ago I read a terrifying news story. A fire had destroyed the second story of the house of a very poor family. The bathroom water heater exploded, and the children were upstairs. Four dead siblings. The smallest a boy of two, the oldest a ten-year-old girl. In the final paragraphs it was reported that the bodies had been found under a bed, in the room where they all slept. It was a detail, a couple of lines at the end, but I couldn't stop imagining the whole scene: the frightened children who didn't know what to do, where to run. Only one place seems able to protect them from the flames. A place that has protected them on other occasions, that at some point has seemed like a stronghold, but that now is a trap. Still, the oldest sister thinks they'll be safe there, or that at least she can calm her brothers and sister by making them think they'll be safe, as they had been in previous situations. The image of the children holding hands, waiting for it all to be over, returns to my mind over and over. Who is to blame? The neighbor who was taking care of them couldn't get up the stairs to rescue them. And the children stayed under the bed, wrapped in flames. What can we think about something like that? Who is responsible, not for the accident, but for the children thinking they would be safe under the bed?

————

The first night Aunt Nana spent with us, my mother came into my room. I heard her climb the stairs, the knocking sound of her square heels that she called classic, but to anyone else were just old-fashioned. Steps that were serious and strong, just as she wanted to be perceived. Footsteps very different from the ones I heard at dawn, when she was barefoot. When she went downstairs around four in the morning, in the dark, carefully, trying not to wake anyone up. In her nocturnal steps there was something she didn't show to anyone, something of fear and submission. I imagined her standing there looking out the window, hidden by the veil of the curtain. I never dared go down and find out what she really did.

My mother turned on the bedside lamp and sat on the bed. "Are you awake?" she asked. I turned toward her. She looked tired, bone-weary. I got the feeling she didn't want to be there, as if someone were forcing her to sit there with me. On many occasions I often felt like something came between us, as if the annoyance were floating in the very air we breathed, inevitable. She merely sat in silence and smoothed the sheets with the palm of her hand.

"Your aunt Nana has always been the same," she said suddenly, with a touch of contempt that, deep down, held a certain admiration. I thought she was going to scold me for shouting at Aunt Nana at breakfast, but she didn't say anything that revealed she knew. Instead, she told me that she'd lived with Aunt Nana until she was five. That her mother had had two daughters very close together and she couldn't take care of both, considering there were three other siblings. That since she was the oldest, she was the one who went with Aunt Nana. I didn't understand what she was getting at;

what concerned me was the coldness of her voice as she spoke to me. She said they'd lived in a very old house with a wooden roof, and that when she had nightmares, Aunt Nana would lie down beside her, and together they counted the knots in the ceiling boards. The game ended when my mother fell asleep. I looked at the ceiling of my room, which was smooth and had some fluorescent stars stuck to it. She sat for a while with her eyes fixed on nothing, silent, and a little while later she said goodbye.

In the doorway she turned around. "Where's your father?" she asked me.

I looked at her without answering.

She sighed deeply and left. She took off her shoes and went to her room in stocking feet.

That night, I couldn't sleep. My mother's visit left me nervous, though I didn't really know why. I'd had trouble sleeping in the past, before school or vacation started, but this time the feeling was different. I felt suffocated, as if the covers on the bed were weighing me down. I wasn't hungry anymore, but the feeling of emptiness only grew. I couldn't stop thinking about my mother as a little girl, small and scared at night. Was that why she went downstairs barefoot in the early morning? Did she also get scared as an adult? I think it was the first time I stayed awake all night; I couldn't stop thinking about those things. I heard my father come home in the early morning hours. I heard the sound of his key chain as he locked all the doors. Then, more silence in the street and the murmur of the bulbs in the streetlamps, the creaking of furniture. The sound returned with the cars and the first rays of sunlight.

The room was flooded with a glacial blue by the time I finally managed to close my eyes.

I got up past ten and went half asleep to my parents' room; the bed was already empty and made. It was Saturday, and silence reigned in the house. I remembered the night before, the conversation with my mother, and I went running to Aunt Nana's room. I needed to apologize for yelling at her. I went through the living room, the dining room, and the kitchen. There was no one there, either. I hadn't entered that room since Sonia had left, and when I did I was surprised; the same white walls looked totally different, as if they were now truly inhabited. There was a lot of furniture, and everything was covered with photos and knickknacks. Old things. One black-and-white photograph caught my attention. The plastic frame was made to look like chrome molding. In the photo, a woman and two little girls were sitting on wooden stools. The adult was without a doubt Aunt Nana. There was her rounded back, her same affable smile and patient expression. Her hair was short and she was wearing a flowered apron. I went closer to try to recognize the other two girls, and then my own face was reflected in the glass. I looked at myself as though in a mirror, but the reflected image didn't look like me, it was like another girl entirely. I looked at her. Her face was gray, ghostly. She didn't even look like a child, more like she was ageless. I felt my chest constrict, and, frightened, I ran to my hideout.

Before going into my room I focus my attention on the sounds of the house. Nothing. The moments I stand on the threshold of my room seem like an eternity. I am completely alone. *Maybe she's not coming back*, I think, and although it's a silly idea since her things are still there, it still upsets me. *I hurt her*, I tell myself, remembering how I'd yelled the morning before. Then, when it all seems like a huge problem, I see something under the bed. It's a gift, but it's not wrapped; there's a ribbon around it and some candies on top. It's a set of cloth handkerchiefs, the kind you carry in your pocket. The box they come in has some Chinese characters on it. I've seen similar ones before, my dad had shown them to me when he worked with the Koreans. A difficult language, he'd said, but to me the characters were more like pictures than words: the outline of a man walking, a house, the branches of a tree. I pick up the handkerchiefs. They're white and embroidered with flowers in pastel colors. I've never received a gift like this before. I hear a door open and close. Someone comes up the stairs, the footsteps are almost imperceptible, as if the person weren't wearing shoes.

"I was at the market," says Aunt Nana, and she comes closer. I'm sitting on the bed, my head down, looking at the handkerchiefs in my hand. "It wasn't easy for me to get under there," she says, laughing and pointing to her curved back.

"I'm sorry," I say, sobbing. She takes one of the handkerchiefs and dries my cheeks. It's rough on the skin and barely gets wet.

"I have several of these," says Aunt Nana. "They've come in handy a lot."

After that, I'm never alone in the house again. I grow up at her side, and she gets old at mine. We found each other, I like to think, the way two children who don't know each other meet freely and play all afternoon, trusting, far removed from caution, from adult suspicion. We watch the soaps, do each other's hair. We make the list for the market: at first I dictate it and she writes, and over time we change roles, because by then it's very hard for her to write. We don't talk much—Aunt Nana is still a silent woman. In any case it isn't necessary, we understand each other perfectly, and silence seems to be precisely the tie that binds us.

We spend the most time in the kitchen, Aunt Nana's habitat. She is clearly comfortable there, in the place where she makes and unmakes with the most freedom, preparing each day's meals and, once a month, her specialty: the walnut kuchen. She knows that she is as safe there as in a bunker, and I also feel protected. There are times when I have the feeling I'm under a giant bed.

At around seven in the evening, my favorite moment of the day begins. Aunt Nana spreads two towels over the table, brings out the basket of clothes, and turns the radio on. She irons. I don't do anything, I'm just there. We always listen to the same program, a kind of radio theater transmitted by the national station. The stories are always suspense and they awaken my curiosity; they fascinate and disturb in equal measure. I'm drawn in by the murders and persecutions, the long and shadowy hallways where two strangers look at each other. I can see us there in the kitchen, not saying anything, immersed in the intrigue of the stories. The air is a bit close because of the iron's steam, and the afternoon light is gradually extinguished almost at the same speed as the narrator tells the story. It all leaves us in shadow, until finally we have to turn the lights on and the radio off.

The kitchen is still our place, but now I am fifteen, then sixteen, and seventeen, and things have changed so much that I don't know to what extent it's still the same rented house, the same family. Or maybe I'm very far from the house and the family. I have two little brothers, a father with occasional jobs, and my mother's nighttime footsteps. Soon I won't have anything.

———

The only thing I maintain more or less intact is my relationship with Aunt Nana. Every night I go to her room and say good night to her with the playful words she taught me when I was seven years old. With her, I go on showing myself as I did when I was little.

Aunt Nana is exhausted. In front of her there's a pile of ironed and folded clothes. The radio program no longer exists. It's almost dark in the kitchen. Tomorrow I'm leaving the house, and aside from some friends who are helping me, no one knows. I haven't told her, I can't open myself up to the possibility of losing any of the courage I need in order to escape. When I was little and cried impotently when I didn't get what I wanted or after fighting with my parents, Aunt Nana always consoled me by saying: "We must be grateful." But the person I am now knows that there's no relief in those words.

Neither of us turns on the light. We stay silent, more so than usual. I think that in reality I don't need to tell her, that in some way she already knows. She looks at me and I see her eyes cloud over with gray—not the gray of rain, but of smoke. It's the last time we are ever together in the kitchen, and her gaze seems like a reply to my decision to escape: "This has been my life, and I understand that not everyone can be grateful." We hug; it's our goodbye.

I knew how it would be. For a while it would be hard to contact me, but still, aside from one call from a public phone, I never visited or contacted Aunt Nana again. Sacrifices, I told myself, and I went on with my life, a life that back then I thought belonged completely to me.

It was only at Aunt Nana's funeral, five years later, that I saw her again. When I arrived, my mother greeted me with a brief and distant "Hello." The wake was held at a funeral home in Independencia, and she was in charge of almost everything: the paperwork, greeting people, offering coffee, tea, cookies, placing the flowers around the room. Later that night, I ran into her outside. I was smoking a cigarette, and she came out to light one too. She had circles under her eyes, and she told me she hadn't held the wake at the house because she didn't live there anymore. I already knew that and I didn't ask any questions, nor did she go on explaining. My father wasn't at the funeral, and I also already knew about that, his absence.

Aunt Nana's dress was navy blue, her favorite color; when I asked, my mother told me she'd chosen it before she died. She told me she had dressed the body, and that she hadn't been able to put Aunt Nana's dentures in because her jaw muscles were too rigid.

"How are you?" she asked. We hadn't spoken since I'd left home.

"Fine," I replied. "And you?"

"Fine."

We were silent, waiting for the cigarettes to burn down. I wanted to talk to her, ask and answer, though I didn't really know what about. As soon as I'd seen her I'd felt like crying, but I held back. I tried to look implacable at all times. Over the years a certain resistance had been forged in me, and there was nothing I could do now to overcome it. Maybe something similar had happened to her.

"She called for your father. Before she died she called his name several times," she said after throwing the butt to the ground. "That's what the nurses told me. She passed away in the early morning, and she'd been talking to herself, calling out for your father."

Nights, I wake up and walk barefoot through the apartment I rent. Tonight, I go into the kitchen and look out the window to the south. Venus is shining above a building's antenna. A year has passed since Aunt Nana died, and I try to imagine her present here, just like in the kitchen of my childhood, rattling the pots and plates in her everyday bustle. I imagine that I'm still in the middle of it all, not doing anything, just being there beside her.

Before the funeral car arrived, the few relatives gathered around the coffin said a few words of farewell. I wanted to say some too, but I couldn't. I wanted to talk about all the things Aunt Nana taught me, and I wanted to talk about silence. Aunt Nana was quiet, and all those afternoons in the kitchen together, she showed me silence, how beautiful it is. That's what I would have liked to say, but I didn't. With my mother there, it didn't seem like the right moment. But more than that, the truth is I said nothing because I didn't dare to speak. It would have meant affirming that I had learned something from her, it would have meant comparing myself with her. And I am different from Aunt Nana. I wasn't like her. I wouldn't have taken responsibility, I wouldn't have done anything she did. And who *could* do that? Worry about everyone's lives but your own. Give yourself to others, be forgotten by others, and be grateful. I was not about to be grateful; at seventeen years old I decided I had to worry about myself. I thought I could leave my family, leave anyone I had to, take off for good and buck the consequences. I had the hope I would be able to forget. I longed for the freedom of a heroine, a life of my own, a happy one. Back then I ridiculously faced down the world, sure I could defeat it and emerge unscathed.

American Spirit

A couple of months ago, I met up with my friend Dorothy. We'd been very close back when we worked at Friday's together, she as a bartender and I as a waitress, but we hadn't seen each other in a long time. Maybe three years, since just after her son was born and I quit. She got in touch through Facebook and suggested we meet up at the old joint in Las Condes, now an Italian restaurant. "To remember the old days," said her message. Not "the good old days" or "the times we had." For her, that period was characterized only by the fact that it had been left behind long ago. I thought I could read a certain detachment in her words that I found odd, but when it came down to it I agreed—that was indeed the best way to define those days.

———

I've never hated a job as much as I hated being a waitress at Friday's. Even so, the afternoon we met up and I saw how the place had changed, I felt nostalgia. The enormous oak bar no longer existed, nor did the propeller that hung over it, or the canoe in the middle of the room, the antiques, the bronze railings, the striped red-and-white tablecloths, the Tiffany lamps. I felt confused. I had cleaned all those things with irritation and deliberate negligence, and here I was now, missing them.

Dorothy was waiting for me, sitting at a table with the menu in her hand. I knelt down beside her the way waiters used to at Friday's in order to create intimacy with the customers, and with that ridiculously fun voice put on to transmit the American spirit, I told her: "Thank God it's Friday."

She smiled a little uncomfortably.

She looked very pretty, different from how I remembered her. She was thinner and her black hair was cut in a bob with bangs, and she wore a vintage blue dress that fit her perfectly.

I told her so:

"You look adorable."

"You look the same," she replied. I guess my expression revealed a certain displeasure, because she immediately backpedaled, saying: "I mean, you're as pretty as ever. As pretty as you always were."

We started catching each other up on our lives. I wasn't particularly satisfied with my present, and I replied with ambiguities and avoided certain subjects. The tricky thing for me, the embarrassing thing, was revealing my generalized failure, especially considering the haughty and idealistic young woman I was when I met Dorothy.

She, on the other hand, happily filled me in about her son, who was two years and eight months old by then, about her relationship of several months with a marine biologist, and her job as an account executive at the Bank of Chile. Her enthusiasm sounded excessive and a little forced. I got the feeling that she wanted to flaunt her achievements to me, though not to make me feel bad. I think that, ultimately, what she needed was approval, a kind of final blessing of her way of life—my blessing. Which is not to say that underneath it she wasn't hiding some resentment.

In our old friendship, I was the one who seemed sure of myself. I'd been nineteen, studying literature, and I was always talking about the subjects I was passionate about and believed to be transcendental: philosophy, politics, cinema, poetry. Dorothy listened to me, insecure and anodyne. She was a few years older than me and worked full-time at the restaurant to help out her family and stay busy at something. She lived with her mom, two aunts, and their daughters in her grandparents' house. Her father was in Miami—he was the one who had chosen that *gringa* name of hers—and his last communication had been when she was in high school (he'd sent her some Incubus CDs).

Waiting tables was good money, but at that time I didn't consider it an occupation to brag about. I said so to Dorothy at the time, and I was always urging her—pressuring her—to study or take an interest in something. I guess I had a very elevated idea of myself, though that was to a large extent a defense mechanism. I lived alone and supported myself, and the thought that I was more than a mere waitress, that I was destined for grander things, gave me the fortitude I needed to bear an exhausting routine and, above all, not go back on my own decisions. It was the life I had chosen when I'd left my parents' home so early.

"I always remember you," said Dorothy, in a tone that seemed too neutral.

I was alarmed at not being able to tell whether the memories she had were good or bad.

Because there was something else underlying it all. When Dorothy got pregnant, her first choice had been to abort, and I'd gone with her to buy the misoprostol, I was beside her when she used it, lying on the bed, too, with my legs elevated and apart, to support her. It didn't work. Most likely they'd sold her false pills, but she decided not to try a second time. She never told me whether she regretted the attempt, but I felt a certain tension when we talked about her son. I thought that deep down, in some hidden and unconscious corner in her heart, she reproached me for having supported her in something that she clearly hadn't wanted. In any case, it would be wrong to say we grew apart because of that. When I disappeared from the map it wasn't because I felt uncomfortable, it was just that I stopped working at the restaurant and I got busy with my own things.

We'd had a good time together. I saved the customers' leftovers so we could eat them in secret, and Dorothy saved the juices and milkshakes from the blender. In the middle of the stress of a full restaurant—"in the weeds," as they say—I'd go running toward the kitchen and tell her "Follow the yellow brick road," or "There's no place like home," and Dorothy would shake her head, laughing. I was sad to feel her so cold now, and for a second I thought about explaining, apologizing if she'd felt that in some way I had been insensitive to her own rhythms and problems. But it would have sounded unjustified and, again, a little arrogant—more conclusions I was drawing about her.

I waved my hand to call the waiter so we could order. There weren't many customers, and the server, around twenty years old, was killing time by polishing the silverware.

"You remember how we used to do that, entertain ourselves polishing silverware?" I asked, trying to guide the conversation toward anecdotes of a much more secure past.

"I don't remember anything 'entertaining' from back then," replied Dorothy. "Really, I don't understand how I stood it for so long in that shitty restaurant."

Her words, like her Facebook messages, surprised me. I never thought Dorothy had a bad aftertaste from the job. Everyone had liked her because she was warm and sociable. She was friends with the other waitresses, and she'd maintained a more or less stable relationship with Diego, the night manager, for years. Along with the cooks, they were a kind of clique, and when the restaurant closed, they used to stay drinking at the bar or go to some after-party. Sometimes they invited me, but I always bowed out saying I had to study or wake up early. The truth is, I didn't go out with them because I thought I'd get bored. They didn't seem interesting enough—people I thought I'd have nothing in common with and nothing to talk about.

"I thought I was the only one who suffered," I told Dorothy, laughing. "Well, me and Denka."

"Denka . . ." said Dorothy, looking to one side and twisting her mouth in an undefinable grimace.

Denka was another night waitress, a student like me. Her real name was Zdenka, she was of Serbo-Croatian descent, and she had a thick nose and red hair and skin. She lived with her mom in an apartment across from Apumanque, so she could allow herself the luxury of a taxi to get home early. She was considered a rich *cuica*, and no one really understood why she worked; clearly, she inspired resentment in those of us who had no choice. That, combined with the fact that she wasn't a particularly likable person—she yelled, complained, and exaggerated—meant she wasn't treated well and had to put up with unpleasant situations.

The general atmosphere in the restaurant wasn't very friendly, or not for everyone. The service industry night shift is a savage and hostile subculture. Many of the waiters did coke when they worked so they could keep up with the pace. And given that the salary was based on tips, the competition was tough and unfair. Friday's was a petty autocracy, which meant that Diego's friends had the best tables and the easiest tasks. That's what I mean when I say I suffered. It was one of my first serious jobs and maybe I blew things out of proportion, but I remember many times when I couldn't take the pressure and I had to lock myself in a cubicle in the employee bathroom to cry. The only thing that consoled me was the thought that all that suffering was temporary. I was only in my first year of college and a professional job seemed far away, and that's why I began to nurse the idea of applying for a literary grant in poetry—a classmate had won one without doing much—that would keep me away from Friday's and any other job. I think I never wanted to be a poet more than I did then.

"Poor Denka," I added, laughing.

My suffering was really nothing compared with Denka's. It wasn't about the tables or the tasks—people made fun of her to her face. The worst part was that for some strange reason, Denka wanted to make friends with all those people who constantly disparaged her. She practically begged to be invited to the after-work parties.

"Why poor?" said Dorothy, and I thought about it.

"Yeah, you're right. In the end she got everyone. She wasn't as dumb as we thought."

Dorothy smiled.

What happened *in the end* was that the restaurant manager fired Diego and one of the waitresses without paying them a cent.

Diego was a forty-something divorcé who liked to party. Not handsome, but roguish. He had a ten-year-old son, and ten years was also more or less how long he'd worked at Friday's. He had started out in the kitchen and worked his way up to night shift manager. His administration wasn't particularly fair, but he won everyone's good graces with the after-parties in the restaurant, when people drank and ate for free—obviously, unbeknownst to the restaurant manager.

The day of his birthday, he planned a special celebration. A real party to which he even invited the day shift waiters. I was off that night, so I didn't even have to invent an excuse. Denka was working, but she wasn't invited. So while everyone else was playing music and setting out bottles of Johnnie Walker on the bar, she was finishing up cleaning the bathrooms before going home.

In the middle of the festivities, at around three in the morning when everyone was pretty drunk, the general manager showed up. He had received an e-mail.

"You remember how crazy that was?"

I remembered those days as long ones, fraught with tension. The manager set about interrogating all the night employees. He threatened mass firings if we didn't give him details about the irregularities that, the e-mail alleged, had been going on for a long time.

"Kind of," said Dorothy. She sat sideways and crossed her legs.

"Luckily, they didn't even ask me anything because the kitchen guys had already spilled it all."

It was true, it had been a relief not to expose myself to the dilemma, especially considering Diego's departure didn't exactly make me sad. I would be well served by a new boss, one who didn't have long-standing friendships and would distribute tables and jobs more fairly.

"Oh, really?" said Dorothy with feigned interest.

The waiter arrived with our order, and after dropping the plates on the tables, he gave a curt "Enjoy."

The manager didn't give away the name of the person who sent the e-mail, but all eyes were on Denka, which led to several regrettable situations. People scrawled things like "Whore!" and "Treacherous bitch!" on her time card, there were shouting matches in the bathroom, and people even threatened violence. Denka went on medical leave for a few weeks due to stress. But when she came back the aggression didn't stop, and finally she quit.

"It's not as if Denka didn't have her reasons," I said. "I even think I envy her a little," I concluded as I twirled fettuccini noodles around my fork.

"You envy her?" asked Dorothy.

I chewed and swallowed quickly.

"I mean, she did something I never would have dared to do. And I'm not saying that because I'm against the parties . . . Considering the late hours, the salary, the terrible conditions and all that, the least they could do was have a little fun. I've always thought you have to stick it to the man a little with these corporate places. Balance things out a little. The problem was Diego—you can't live in a glass house and also treat people unfairly. Someone's going to end up making you pay, right? Everything in life comes back to you," I declared in a know-it-all tone.

"Everything in life comes back to you . . ." repeated Dorothy. She leaned toward me, rested her elbows on the table, and pointed her fork at me. "Do you really think Denka would have dared do something like that?" she asked, looking me in the eyes.

"Who else?"

She leaned back in her chair again and clasped her hands.

"Well," she said, widening her eyes, "Denka wasn't the only one who had something against Diego . . ." She let the words float in the air as she cocked her head to the side and bit her lips.

"*You* sent that mail?"

Dorothy nodded, smiling.

"Are you joking?" I asked her, and I burst out laughing.

She gave me a defiant look.

"But why? How? Why?" I asked. The office workers two tables down turned to look at me.

"Let's just say it was revenge," she explained serenely. "You remember how I used to go out with Diego?"

"Yeah, that's why I don't get it."

"Diego was 'unfair,' as you say. But not just at work," she said, forcing a mysterious tone. Then she was silent for a while.

"But what happened?" I said. "They kicked him to the curb without paying him a cent. You could have ended up fired, too. All of us could have," I said, trying not to sound reproachful. "Didn't you care?"

"They weren't going to fire anyone else, they just said that to pressure people. Do you really think they would get rid of their whole night shift from one day to the next?"

"No, but—"

"You remember Lisette?" she asked. "She worked the lunch shift."

"No. Not really."

"Well. The thing is that, out of the blue, Diego told me he wanted to try again with his ex-wife. He said he needed to give it one last chance. He told me he wasn't doing it for himself, but for his son, to give him a family. It broke my heart, but of course I understood and told him not to worry, that I'd be there for him, I'd support him . . . But then, a little before his birthday, I found out he'd been screwing Lisette for months. The line about going back to his wife was never true."

She paused and took a sip of beer. Then she went on:

"I felt awful, of course. And I suffered and cried and all that. But it also made me furious, really furious. And, well, I didn't want to sit around and wait for the world to pay him back," she finished in a provocative tone.

Dorothy looked at me defiantly, and I at her, admiring. The kind of admiration I feel for villains, with their brave and intelligent plans. Though Dorothy was no villain, no vigilante. The role she had played was more complex than that.

"Does anyone else know?"

"No. It's my secret."

I took a long sip of beer. I looked around in search of anything

I could recognize from the old Friday's dining room. All those people I'd thought were so insignificant came back to my mind, now the protagonists of my memories. Denka's eyes filled with fear, Diego's with resignation and sadness. Even though I never saw him in person, I even imagined Diego's son, the ten-year-old boy with his unemployed father. Over all those faces in my mind emerged Dorothy's, impassive. She hadn't been part of the chorus of suspects when it all happened. I tried to remember how she'd acted, what her reaction had been. Was she upset or scared? Tired and sad? Silent and doubtful, or was there a triumphant glint in her eyes? Something in me refused to accept that she'd been capable of sending that e-mail. That she had woven such a plot and borne the pressure of the consequences.

"You know the funniest thing about it?" asked Dorothy, interrupting my thoughts. "It was thanks to you. You played a very important role."

I looked at her, confused.

"You remember that book you lent me?"

"What book?"

"Remember how you were always talking about books, and sometimes I asked you to lend me one?"

I said yes, but the truth is I didn't remember lending her books, much less her asking for them.

"I don't remember what it was called. You told me it was short and I could read it fast, but I gave it back to you, like, a year later because I read it really slow. And you remember that weird Korean movie you made me watch? You burned me a DVD of it, remember, and I told you I didn't like it, that it was really messed up?" She paused and took a sip of beer. "Well, I guess in the end I liked it, I liked them. The book and the movie. I don't know, they were about revenge, and I was reading the book when this all went down . . . I guess they influenced me somehow. Or at least they gave me permission to be angry and act according to my feelings. You know?"

"Yeah, I get it," I replied. And although it still struck me as twisted, it was true. I did understand her.

Finally, I understood her. I realized I had underestimated her. I'd always looked down on her, thinking she was as innocent and loyal as she was indifferent and cowardly.

After dessert, we hugged goodbye and promised we would get together more often. For her son's birthday, or when a good movie was playing. We never talked again. And not because of Dorothy's confession. I think we both accepted there is nothing tying us together anymore. Our friendship was circumstantial, though no less genuine for that. It must be the same with firefighters: in the heat of the moment they're ready to give their lives for one another, and afterward they go drink a couple beers, but that doesn't mean they're going to spend New Year's together or even that they have much in common. Maybe the only thing we still had pending was that episode. And after our last meeting, it became just one more anecdote from the *old days*.

That afternoon I walked from El Golf to Plaza Italia. I walked quickly down Isidora Goyenechea and looked for a way to cut over to the park that runs along the Mapocho. On the way I saw a young priest; a woman using a metal detector; a man with a guitar on his shoulder and a tattoo on his arm of a woman with a clock for a head. Anyone I passed would have seemed strange and meaningful.

I was moved, not by Dorothy's story itself, but because I thought it worked as a perfect metaphor. It's what has been happening to me lately, now that I'm twenty-five. Revelations. Disillusionment. I felt like someone just starting to understand how the world works, someone gullible and clean, a victim. And I guess my eyes stayed wide and naïve for several days after that. Aggrieved before the world's mocking smile.

Then I remembered a couple more things.

One in particular.

I must have been working at Friday's about a year and a half when this happened. A weekday, an average day. I was waiting on a gringo couple. They must have been over sixty years old and seemed to be married. They were very friendly and talkative, and at a certain moment the husband got up and asked me where the bathroom was. I told him I'd show him, and as we walked through the restaurant's dining room, he took me by the hand. I was surprised, and then I looked at our hands. I must have looked closely at his, because I remember he was wearing a big ring with a blue stone on his ring finger, and that the texture of his skin, in spite of the wrinkles, was soft. I was surprised, it infuriated me, I felt sad, but I let him take my hand. And I did it for the tip, because he was a gringo and gringos always left good tips, and because I assumed, in that brief moment when I looked at his hand over mine, that if I showed my annoyance he wouldn't leave one. So I let an old man take my hand, for money.

It may seem ridiculous, but I've never told that to anyone. I could have told Dorothy that day we met for lunch—it would have offset her story and evened out our experiences. But I didn't. And it wasn't because I was ashamed—which *is* the reason I've never shared that story—but simply because I wasn't thinking about it during our meal. I didn't remember. I guess that's how it works. It's not about being naïve; what you do is fool yourself, and you do it so well that one day your actions come back to you and take you by surprise, sneak up behind you. Or that's what I think now, as I once again wander with no fixed direction. I have to hold on to that idea, because I'd rather play the wise guy than come off as wide-eyed.

Laika

osefa woke up from a brief dream. In the darkness, someone was shaking her shoulder, gently but insistently. Someone was saying her name, whispering. "Josefa, Josefa, wake up."

"Hi, Fede," she replied in a sleepy voice.

"Hi, Josefa," he said. She could barely see his face as she reached out her hand to be sure he was there; he caught it and kissed her open palm. "We're going to the beach to see UFOs," said Fede.

"I'm sleepy," she said, and now she could see him in the darkness of the room. She loved that, how her eyes could adjust to the night like a cat's.

"Come on, kiddo," Fede insisted, and when he said it she felt afraid. Fede's eyes shone like a sky full of UFOs.

"I'm scared," said Josefa.

"It's all right, UFOs are as harmless as the stars," he soothed her, "and plus, you're with me." Her mother had told her to behave with Fede, because the Argentines were going to help them. Josefa didn't want to make her mother look bad, or to disobey her. Lately her mother had been scolding her a lot, and she didn't want to get into any more trouble. She didn't want to disappoint her anymore.

"Can I bring my shovel?" asked Josefa, still a bit unsure. It wasn't a toy plastic shovel, but a real one, a metal one her mother used for gardening and that Josefa had begged to borrow, to bring with her on vacation. An adult tool. Josefa's dream was to become an adult quickly, wake up one day and realize that she was a grown-up and could do all the things adults did, or that she thought adults did, like use a metal shovel and not a plastic one.

"Sure," said Fede, smiling. "You never know when it might come in handy."

Josefa pointed him to where it was. He pulled the covers off her, picked up the shovel from the nightstand, and knelt down, holding it horizontally in his hands as if he were offering her a sword. Josefa took it, laughing, and held it tightly. "See, I'm a real knight-errant," said Fede, and he wrapped her in a blanket and picked her up, feeling his way in the darkness.

At that early morning hour the beach was deserted. Fede said that if they were going to see a UFO they'd have to get as far away as possible from civilization. He crossed the rock bed that edged the cabins to reach a small deposit of sand. Cradled in his arms like that, Josefa could see part of Fede's profile against a starry background. Still holding her he sat down in the sand, then tilted his head back to look at the sky.

Several minutes passed and Fede stayed in the same position, thoughtful and silent, maintaining a certain gravity, as if to add scientific authority to the matter. If it hadn't been for the cold, Josefa would have fallen asleep.

"Look," said Fede suddenly. He pointed up, and his index finger followed a luminous ball as it slowly crossed the sky. Josefa clutched the shovel more tightly and brought it to her chest and started to tremble, although not out of fear of the UFO, but because she was cold.

Fede lit a cigarette. "Josefa," he said very seriously, "I'm not going to lie to you. I would love it if we saw one together, but that's not a UFO, it's a satellite. See how it's moving? It's an artificial satellite that circles Earth. There are lots of them. Some are old and don't even work, they just orbit without a purpose. They're what's called space debris. There's another one, see it?"

Josefa saw it.

"Are they like Laika?" she asked, pointing at the sky.

"Oh!" Fede said approvingly. "You know about Laika! I always said you weren't just another pretty kid." He kissed her on the nose, and she smelled his tobacco breath. Josefa laughed shyly. If she knew about Laika it was only because of the song by Mecano that her mother listened to. She loved that song. It seemed so mysterious, and when she listened to it she was filled with questions. What had become of Laika? Where was she now? Did she know she was famous, and there was a song in her honor? There were a lot of things that seemed mysterious to her; the world held secrets that no one knew or understood: ships and planes that got lost in the Bermuda

Triangle. The Egyptian pyramids. The disappearance of the Mayans and the dinosaurs. Fire. Ants. Rasputin surviving poison and bullets. Marylin's murder. Michael Jackson's skin. Josefa believed that when she died and went to heaven, God, or one of his angels, would clear up all of these great enigmas, and sometimes her wish to know was so great that she wanted to be dead, to die just for a little while.

"You know what the spaceship they sent Laika up in was called?" asked Fede, exhaling smoke.

Josefa shook her head. She worried that Fede would realize that she really didn't know much more about Laika.

Once, when she was in kindergarten, a teacher had asked, "Who knows how to draw a star?" Josefa raised her hand along with all the other kids and went to the blackboard, smiling and confident, and with the chalk she drew a kind of circle with points. All the kids laughed and shouted that that wasn't a star, and then Josefa looked at the chalkboard again and realized it was true, that what she had drawn wasn't what she'd seen in her mind, it wasn't a star. In the afternoon, at Mauricio's house, she started to cry. Mauricio was the son of the neighbor who took care of her in the afternoons, and he consoled her, telling her not to worry, that he would teach her the easiest way to draw a star. First she had to draw an inverted V, then an upward line to the left, another horizontal line to the right, and finally a downward one to meet the initial point of the V. "It draws itself, see?" said Mauricio. "And you don't even have to lift the pen." That was another reason Josefa wanted to be an adult. If she learned how to draw stars and do all the other things adults knew how to do, no one would laugh at her again.

———

"*Sputnik Two.* A Soviet ship," said Fede, delighted with his own words. "Laika was a mutt, a street dog. Her real name was Kudryavka, and she beat the other two dogs the Russians were training. She was the first living being to travel in space, and after seven hours, the first to die in orbit."

Josefa didn't like hearing that Laika was dead. Really, it was pretty stupid on her part to think the dog could still be alive, flying around out in space, but that's how she'd imagined her, just like in the song, looking out through the rocket's window at the colored ball that was Earth.

"She's carved beside Lenin on the Monument to the Conquerors of Space. There's a poem on the monument. One verse says, 'We have forged great flaming wings.' In Russian, of course. I like the Russians more than the Yankees, how about you?"

Huddled in Fede's arms, Josefa said she preferred the Russians too, but she didn't really know what that meant, and she said it in a voice so quiet it was as if she'd said nothing at all.

Fede knew a lot of things, she thought. Just like Mauricio. Although they knew different things. What Mauricio knew mostly had to do with superhero stories. She liked Fede, same as Mauricio. But Mauricio didn't hug her like Fede did. In fact, Mauricio almost never hugged her, what he did was take her arms and make her hit herself in the face with her own hands while he asked her, "Why are you hitting yourself?" or attack her with tickles until she couldn't take it anymore. And one time, she hadn't been able to stand it and she'd peed her pants, and Mauricio had laughed for like two hours, until she'd started crying from shame. Then he told her to go to the bathroom and take off her wet underwear so he could wash them and dry them with the hair dryer, and that's what happened, and when her mother came to pick her up that night, Mauricio didn't say anything, he didn't tell on her for peeing her pants.

"I'd love to study astronomy. I graduate from high school this year, but I'm not doing so well. And astronomy is a really hard major, I wouldn't have the head for it," admitted Fede, a little gloomily. "And, well, it looks like we're not going to see UFOs today."

Josefa giggled at his accent, so Argentine and exaggerated.

"What're you laughing at? You laughing at me, midget?" said Fede, teasing. "Let's see, stand up, let's just see how tall you are. I bet you don't even come up to my knees."

Josefa laughed again, and Fede threw his cigarette into the sand.

"Litter bug!" she said, growing more confident.

"What do you mean, litter bug? Who're you calling a litter bug?" He let her tumble from his arms into the sand, took the shovel away from her, and stuck it into the sand behind him. Then he took Josefa under the armpits and stood her up in front of him.

"Let's see, let me look at you," he said, bringing his hand to his chin as if in doubt. He pulled off the blanket that covered her.

"Do you like me?" he asked her, his hand still on his chin, his eyes half closed.

Josefa looked down at the sand and nodded.

"How much do you like me? From here to the moon?"

She nodded again. She thought Fede was the cutest boy on the face of the earth, as cute as the leading men on TV, or her father in old photos from when he was young.

"I like you from here to Pluto," he said, and he lifted her face with his hand so she would look him in the eyes. "There and back."

"What about Paola?"

"Paola? Who's Paola?"

"From cabin nine."

"That kid doesn't know anything, not like you. You know all about the space age." Fede winked at her. Josefa couldn't contain her joy.

"Plus, she doesn't know how to kiss, and you do."

Josefa's face lit up. It was true, she did know how.

"Have you given a lot of kisses?"

She nodded over and over, excited.

TV kisses. She practiced on her dad and her mom, suctioning with her lips and moving her head from side to side, like the protagonists did.

Fede slowly moved closer and took the girl's little head in his hands. His breathing was agitated. He closed his eyes and placed his lips on Josefa's, and she blinked nervously. She was about to start with her head movements when she felt a soft cone, damp and cold, penetrate her mouth. She opened her eyes wide and she couldn't move her head, she practically couldn't move a muscle with the surprise of the tongue. She didn't know that part, they didn't show it on TV.

Fede pulled away.

"Hmmm," he said, sounding disappointed. "You've still got some learning to do."

Josefa lowered her head and felt like crying.

"No, kiddo, don't take it like that," he said, raising her head with his fingers. "It was really good for how little you are." Josefa was relieved. "Plus, I can teach you. You have to imitate what I do in there. So when we get married you'll be an expert kisser."

She opened her eyes wide as saucers again.

"Because you *do* want to marry me, right?"

Josefa nodded vigorously.

Fede unclasped the chain he wore around his neck.

"Like it?" he asked, showing her the golden sun hanging from the chain. "This will be the symbol of our engagement." He put it around her neck. "When you turn eighteen, I'm going to come to Chile to find you and we'll get married." He gave her another kiss, but this time shorter, without tongue; a brief aspiration, like the ones Josefa's parents gave each other. She knew other kids were grossed out when their parents kissed, but she loved it, even if on the rare occasions that they did, it was like that: no head movements, as if in passing.

Josefa took the sun between her hands. She looked at it as though hypnotized, and she puffed out her chest to show it off better.

"Now we have to seal our pact in the ocean," said Fede, looking at the water. He tied Josefa's wavy hair back with an elastic band. "You don't want to catch cold on vacation from going to bed with wet hair," he said, smiling, and he started to undress her. First her pajama top. It was yellow, her favorite color, with an embroidered elephant holding a half-melted ice cream cone. Then her socks, and finally her pants.

Josefa's chest caved in and she blushed, and the sun sank along with her chest. All of her sank.

Naked in front of Fede, Josefa felt ashamed again, but it was a different shame from what she felt when she saw the badly drawn star on the classroom chalkboard. It was more like the emotion that came over her when they'd given vaccinations at school. She'd moved along in the line of children, shyly, because she knew that everyone would see her half naked when she took off her uniform blouse, but she was also eager to do it. It was a disappointment when her turn with the nurse came and she only unbuttoned the sleeve and rolled it up above her elbow.

"That little belly is mine," said Fede, stroking Josefa's prominent stomach. He kissed her belly button and again farther up. A kiss with tongue on her nipple, and when his mouth separated from her skin, Josefa saw a little thread of shining saliva that joined her body and Fede's lips like a spider's silk. A shiver ran over her body, like when her mother was braiding her hair and accidentally pulled a few solitary hairs.

Fede pulled her to him and hugged her very tightly and licked her neck like it was a stamp. "You taste like sunscreen," he said, "beach flavor."

He took off his pants, his jacket, shirt, and underwear, quickly. And Josefa looked at the parts of his body that weren't so tanned, and his erect penis that pointed toward the ocean like the needle of a compass. She had never seen one before and she was fascinated. From then on, that would be her image of penises. Not fallen and flaccid like her father's, which she would see one day when she opened the bathroom door and surprised him coming out of the shower, but rather straight and firm. Implacable, like the broomstick her mother used to clear the plums off the porch. Perpetual like the hands of the watches she drew on her left wrist when she was bored in class.

They walked to the water hand in hand. And Josefa thought that they were like Adam and Eve in her children's Bible, which she read from every night. Her favorite story was Samson and Delilah, because it was the most romantic.

As she walked, she turned back and looked at their footprints. The marks in the dry sand, shallow and imprecise. The marks in the wet sand, more detailed, reflecting the difference in their weights and sizes. They would all be erased soon and would go back to being part of the beach. Some sooner than others, but they would all disappear. When Josefa saw them she realized that everything she was experiencing with Fede was real. It sometimes happened that she had very vivid memories from when she was little that later turned out to be dreams or inventions, confusions of hers. There were two in particular. In the first one she was with her mother, and they were home alone at night. She woke up to some strange noises, and she called to her mother. Together they went into the living room, and in the darkness there they saw the thieves. They were hidden, crouched down under the dining room table, behind the sofas, the gas heater. There must have been four of them, and Josefa remembered seeing the outline of their black uniforms with the high collars of thieves, and how they seemed like children playing hide-and-seek. The other memory was of an afternoon she spent with her father. She couldn't picture very well what they were doing, but at one point he'd told her that he had the power to disappear, and he went running to the bedroom. She followed him, but when she got there, he wasn't there. She looked for him all over the room, and then all through the rest of the house, but she couldn't find her father. Then she sat down in front of the mirror, and while she looked at herself and played at tracing the outline of her flat reflection, she came to the conclusion that her father had drunk a potion like in Alice in Wonderland, to shrink down to a tiny size and hide. The images of those memories were very clear in her mind, even clearer than others that actually happened. They had gradually lost their authenticity as she'd gotten bigger, when they no longer seemed logical or possible, and she had to force herself not to call them up.

But there were the footprints, two pairs for two people. Some the wind would erase, and others the sea. They wouldn't be permanent, they would pass into oblivion like everything, and that made them real.

They went out until the water covered his chest and they let themselves be rocked by the calm sea. He hugged her from behind and sucked on her neck like the mollusks on the rocks all around them. "I'm in love," he repeated. "I'm crazy for you."

Josefa's eyes were on the horizon. The sea and the sky seemed to her a single darkness, just as the world of Genesis must have been, before God separated the waters that were above the firmament from those below it.

The sea and the sky were a single darkness, and the UFOs could just as well be above as below, flying and floating at the same time.

Last Vacation

What I'm going to relate here happened the last summer of my childhood, or what I understand to be my childhood, a sort of instinctive or unconscious state that came before my life changed and took on a definitive direction. Before my older brother lost his left foot, before I went to stay with my mom for good and dropped out of school, before all the other things that led me down the path to what my life is now. A destiny that seemed clear to everyone around me—and one they didn't consider at all good—but one that, in the end, I made the decision to follow. That's why it makes sense to me to tell about that summer vacation. I think it was that trip, to a large extent, that shaped my decision, though I was unaware of it at the time.

I'm talking about the summer vacation of 2010, when I was ten years old and went to La Serena with my aunt Veronica and her two daughters, Camila and Javiera.

La Serena: It strikes me now as the most incredibly apt name for the days I spent there. The first memory that comes to mind is the sensation of floating there in my underwear in the warmest waters I'd ever felt, looking up at the sky and the imperceptible movement of the clouds. *Serenity*, and other words like it, had been a blank space in the dictionary of my life.

Up until that summer I had spent my childhood without a fixed home, moving back and forth between my mother's and grandmother's houses. My mom owned an apartment in the Parinacota projects, in Quilicura. A small social housing apartment—which the government traded her for a savings account with one hundred thousand pesos in it—where there was almost never food or water; the stove and the pipes had been stolen during a few weeks when the apartment had stood empty. So we would sleep there at night, when there was no hunger or need to bathe, and the rest of the time we were at my grandmother's house. I also stayed with my grandmother on weekends and the days when my mom disappeared. Sometimes my older brother Mauri was there too, but most of the time I was alone, because my brother had also started to disappear without warning. I called my grandma "Mami" and my mother "Mama," and I had similar names for my grandfather and my dad, though my dad was practically a stranger to me because he'd been in prison since I was a baby.

Mama and Mami. They both loved me, but they were hard women. You couldn't imagine them whispering. My grandmother was a fat woman with the face of an Arab. She spent her whole life working a stall in the market, and as an old woman she converted and became an evangelist. She called my mother "this one" or "the dummy" and said that she was God's way of punishing her. She never mentioned, though, what he was punishing her for. She used to tell the story of my mother's conception as if it were the omen of her downfall: she'd already had five children and was old to have another, but after a botched operation to remove her wisdom teeth she'd had to take antibiotics, and they had neutralized her birth control pills.

My mother's name was Karen. She was dark-skinned, with frizzy black hair and squinty eyes. Her flaccid body and spotted, wrinkled face made her look like a fifty-year-old woman, though she was only a little over thirty. My grandmother said she had no right to complain, given the "low" way she'd lived her life. My mother had gotten married at seventeen, had two sons and largely abandoned them, and then she met my father and had me. Today, in spite of her record, I don't think of her as having been particularly intense. Rather, she was someone who simply didn't care much about things, who lived each day according to her own rhythm.

Physically, I looked a lot like my mama, though I was even more squinty-eyed. And, as a kid that age does, I understood that my whole being was tied to her and her life. But unlike my grandmother, I didn't see that as punishment. My mother and my family life seemed completely normal to me. It was normal for her not to work, or for me not to see her for days at a time, or to see her drunk or in a shouting match with my grandmother. It was normal that my brother had only made it to second grade and barely knew how to read or write, or that he had a record with child protective services. I didn't feel confused or abandoned, and I didn't suffer any more than a kid who doesn't get what he wants for Christmas. But I guess that in the eyes of my aunt Veronica, my mama's older sister, I must have seemed vulnerable. And maybe it was as a kind of restitution that she took me on vacation to La Serena in the first place.

We stayed at a campground called Las Licitas, some thirty kilometers north of the city and almost totally isolated by dunes and rocks. They chose a site looking out over the coast for the three tents they'd brought, two bedrooms and a kitchen. It wasn't that they especially liked to camp, as I'd assumed; rather, it was what they could afford, and they preferred to pay less and spend almost a month with the beach a couple of steps away. The day we arrived, they set up the tents while I went to play on the beach. I didn't even put on swim trunks, I ran in my underwear to get my first taste of the ocean they'd told me so much about on the way there. I noticed that the underpants embarrassed them a little, but I also realized they let me be. I'm sure they saw me as a little animal, as wild as he was wounded, who needed to be indulged. I saw them as three total strangers, but they seemed to know a lot about me, who I was and where I came from.

On the trip there, during the few hours I'd been awake—my aunt liked to get the jump on the day, so we started off around five in the morning—I'd entertained them with the novelty of me. My aunt drove, Camila was in the passenger seat, and Javiera and I rode in back. My head between the seats, I said some words in the Creole I'd learned from my Haitian neighbors. They complimented my skill, which was what I was after, but a little while later my aunt asked me if there were many foreigners living in our building and, a few minutes later, if it was dangerous. She said she'd read an article that mentioned Parinacota as drug dealer territory. "Quilicura, dangerous?" I asked, laughing. Wanting to go on dazzling them, I told them how no one messed with us, how in the projects we were "respected," and my punch line was about how when we went to the mall—me, Mama, and Mauri—the guards would follow us around. My aunt turned serious. She slowed the car and turned down the radio. She told me it wasn't good to brag about that, a person had to try to be decent, as decent as possible, and that she and her daughters were decent people. I didn't know what to say, and there was an uncomfortable silence that Javiera dissolved by asking me what I wanted to listen to on the radio. "Reggaeton!" I shouted with willful enthusiasm, to make them see I hadn't lost a drop of my joy, or the confidence that went with it.

My aunt Veronica was the polar opposite of my mother. Though she wasn't the oldest, she'd been the first of the sisters to get married, leave the neighborhood, and distance herself from poverty and the family in almost every possible sense. She'd separated from her husband a few years before, worked in a bank, and had a modern apartment that was comfortable and clean. She was very pretty, with white skin and dyed blond hair. She looked much younger than she was, much younger than Mama. From the start, she was always affectionate and attentive with me. She couldn't understand how they'd sent me with only one change of clothes for the whole vacation, and our second day there she took me to the mall in La Serena. She bought me underwear, socks, two pairs of jeans, a pair of shorts, T-shirts, and a plaid button-down. She chose everything. The two of us went in the morning, and when we were on the way back she asked me if Mama had forgotten to pack my bag. I dodged the question. The answer was: partly yes, partly no. My mom had disappeared some days before the trip, and those were the only clothes I had at my grandmother's house; she was the one who'd packed my bag. My aunt's voice took on that serious tone, precise as a clock, that she used sometimes when she talked to me; she told me that if my mom didn't take care of those things, then I would have to do it myself. I had to learn that I was the only person responsible for me. I nodded, accepting the challenge, and my aunt switched to a sweeter tone and asked me if I liked my new clothes. I just said "thank you" and turned to look out the window. We were driving along the highway and I couldn't see the ocean, just dunes and some plants that looked dead. The landscape didn't vary from one kilometer to the next. I thought of my house. The project where I lived with Mama was just as desertlike, it didn't have any green either, but it was always so full of people, teeming and sonorous, it would never seem dead. I didn't understand why the issue of the clothes was a problem. My sweat suits were my favorite articles of clothing, I only took them off so they could be washed. I had one set that was knockoff Adidas, another that was real Puma. Mama had gotten them for me; she loved sweat suits and sports clothes, too.

Though she would never have said it, my aunt was most likely thinking the words *low class* as she picked out clothes for me. During that summer she did her utmost to please and advise the smiling, talkative, and entertainingly bold boy that I was, and ultimately I let myself be loved, I accepted her good intentions naturally, though at first I acted defensively. I distrusted that affection that seemed to come out of nowhere, and I resisted her criticism. I was very sure of myself, I was happy with the life I led, and I didn't think I needed her words or her help.

The first night, after an entire day of playing on the beach, my aunt sent me to off to the campground's showers. I didn't want to go, but I obeyed. When I got there, I felt uneasy. My heart pounded in my chest, and a strange fear came over me. At home, to avoid my grandmother's complaints about the water or gas bills, I almost always showered with my mother or brother, sometimes all three of us together. And while one person washed their hair, the other scrubbed with a washcloth, and we played, spitting water or throwing soap suds. We shared an intimacy that, I guess, comes with poverty. This shower was exclusively for me, and it was so far from them, my family, that it was perhaps the first time I really felt abandoned.

I slept in an old A-shaped tent. Though it was out of style then and had a pitched roof that didn't handle the coastal winds very well, it was everything a kid imagines as "camping." I shared it with Javiera, the older of my two cousins, who was twenty-five. To me, she was the prettiest of the three. More so now, idealized in my memory, just like the A-shaped tent.

I had a crush on Javiera, and during that summer she was a kind of role model for me, the way friends' older siblings often are, or certain teachers. She seemed beautiful and mysterious to me.

Back then I wouldn't have used this word, but now I think it's the one that best describes how I saw her: *dark*. Inside as well as out. Her thin, curveless body, her pallid skin, her gray eyes, black hair, and her nails painted navy blue—all those things were little reflections of her personality. Silent, solitary, hermetic.

I also preferred her over my aunt and Camila because she didn't place demands on me. Not directly, at least. She was uncomfortable when her mother and sister went off on their sermons, and she always tried to change the subject. She gave the impression she didn't think she was one to give advice to anyone, though that was largely because of how sad she was. Dejected. All I knew about the matter was what I'd heard from my grandmother one afternoon. She said Javiera's boyfriend had dumped her, and that after she'd been gone for six years, she'd come home "with her tail between her legs." An image that at the time didn't seem at all sad to me, but really funny.

Javiera was the first woman to captivate me. Out of nowhere, she'd caress my hair or kiss my cheek, and then she wouldn't pay any attention to me for the rest of the day—an infallible feminine maneuver that I was experiencing for the first time. It was clear she'd once been a girl who knew all the tricks, but now she was sad. Her mother and younger sister were very close; they slept in the other tent and talked late into the night. Javiera always looked at them as if they had just scolded her. Maybe I identified with her because of that: like me, Javiera seemed leery.

She called me Nicolai or Nicolaia, for the characters in the Chekhov stories she was reading. She asked me if I knew what my name meant, and I, who of course had no idea, shrugged my shoulders. "It's a glorious name," she said. "It means victory of the people," and she added that she'd always thought Chekhov used that name ironically for his characters because of the tsar. Also, that the very fact that the tsar was named Nicolas and ended up as he did was ironic. I went on shrugging, not understanding a word. She'd brought two books for me: *The Adventures of Sherlock Holmes* and *Aesop's Fables*. The fables had illustrations and very little text; the other was what I thought of as a "real" book then, with more than two hundred pages and no pictures. Javiera said she didn't know which one was more appropriate for my age, so she'd brought them both. My aunt voiced the opinion that a Harry Potter book would have been ideal, and Javiera looked disgusted. She'd studied literature.

We had an agreement: I would read out loud to her every night in exchange for five hundred pesos. A spectacular deal for me, who tended to move around with fifty- and ten-peso coins. Javiera understood how the world worked, and that I wasn't a boy she could convince with candies. My plan was to save it all and return to Santiago with ten thousand pesos in my pocket.

The first night, while Javiera was brushing her teeth, I picked up the book of fables, and when she came back I told her I'd finished it. "The whole thing?" she asked in surprise. I nodded, smiling, and I showed her the morals highlighted in purple squares at the end of each fable. "Clever!" she said. "But you skipped the stories."

"But the part in the squares is the most important," I argued. "The rest is just filling." She laughed and said that the moral depended on the story, you couldn't understand them separately. "I understood everything," I assured her.

"Mmmm . . . really, I guess it's a brilliantly practical method . . . But that's not what reading is about . . . you have to waste a little time." And she opened the book for me to start reading from the beginning.

Practical. I like to think about the boy I was then as a practical person. I guess to a certain extent I was; I didn't sweat things, my world didn't collapse when there were problems. I adapted, I think that's the best word. I didn't complain, and I adapted. But nor would it be true to say that I didn't care about things, or that they didn't affect me. Giving the appearance of adapting—that was the way to keep safe, it was the bulletproof vest I wore under my clothes. "Clever," Javiera called me. "Naughty," others had said before. "Liar," I knew.

Javiera changed my relationship to books. They had passed through my hands before—we had required readings every two months at school—but this was a different kind of obligation. I was a very good reader for my age, at least compared with my classmates. It was easy for me, though I found it boring. So at first, to make it fun, I put on the voices of the characters the way I imagined them, or I read in a singsong voice, following or forcing a certain musicality in the words. Javiera laughed, but the jokes weren't enough for her, and at the end of every reading session she asked me a series of questions that I couldn't answer because I'd retained only the sound of the words. So then I had to make an effort and concentrate on the meaning of each of the sentences. I had to chew them, not just taste their flavor. In reality, I didn't do it so much for the money, but because it seemed important to Javiera, and I didn't want to disappoint her. I wanted her to keep seeing me as a clever boy.

That was my path to books. Maybe it's not very romantic, but I guess that's how it happens with some readers: we're recruited by a challenge. The books they made me read in school didn't challenge me, but the ones Javiera brought me did. Reading was like putting together a jigsaw puzzle, or, as in the Sherlock Holmes adventures, like being a detective. There was something hidden, a lost piece, and you couldn't always find it, and maybe it didn't even exist.

Her method wasn't exactly pedagogical. She bombarded me with questions, what did this or that mean in the story, when I barely understood what it meant for one thing to mean something else besides what it was. I felt pressured and a little intimidated, but as it became a habit, I started to like the little ritual of reading at night. Eventually I almost wanted the day to end, so Javiera would pull the lamp closer and we would climb into the tent. Something happened as I read beside her, a different atmosphere was created, a kind of intimacy.

Now I think that making me read was her way of guiding me, an indirect way that was more complicated than my aunt's. "Morals." "Deductive reasoning." It seems pretty obvious, but the truth is that meaning is never as simple as it seems. When she made me read, Javiera wasn't telling me "You're on the wrong path, you have to take this other one," but something more like: "There are many paths, and when the moment comes to decide which to take, it's best to be prepared." Sherlock Holmes criticized Watson for something similar, reducing his cases from academic courses to adventure tales. Watson, like Javiera, knew that sometimes it's much easier, maybe more beneficial, to put oneself in another's skin than to memorize a mathematical formula.

In any case, it's possible that those weren't Javiera's intentions, and this is just something I think now, after having read many more books and coming to think of that vacation as a milestone in my life.

I read at night, and Javiera read in the mornings.

While my aunt went to the market or the port to buy food for lunch and Camila was still asleep in the tent, Javiera and I went down to the beach, which at that hour was almost deserted. I wore my bathing suit and carried my towel and bucket, and Javiera had her *Selected Stories* and her cigarettes.

In La Serena it always dawned cloudy, and the landscape took on a melancholic pallor. Even the dunes, which burned under the sun during the rest of the day, seemed languid in the mornings. Javiera read leaning against an umbrella with a wooden shaft buried in the sand. I looked at her from the shore while I gathered shells to take to Mama and Mami. Leaning over the book, her hair forming a tent around the pages, she seemed separate from everything.

"Look, a dog," I said one morning, pointing to a wooly mutt by her feet.

"Yep," she said, looking up at me as I stood there soaking wet. "Like the fable of the wolf and the dog."

"But this is a free dog, he's not chained up at night," I rushed to say. I was eager to impress her with intelligent comments. The one about the dog was something I'd had stored away since I'd seen this one wandering around a few days before.

"Exactly, my dear Nicolai," she said, smiling, and since I couldn't think of anything else to say to attract her attention, we were silent for a long time, and she went back to her book.

I didn't want her to go back into her shell, I wanted to talk to her, about anything. I blurted out the first thing to come into my head: "Why were you crying yesterday?"

Since I wasn't used to it, the sound of waves breaking often woke me up in the middle of the ocean. But the night before, in addition to the thundering water, I'd heard a sobbing that was faint, but just as deep as the ocean's.

Javiera blushed and looked down.

"Is it the mattress?" I asked. I was sleeping on a very comfortable inflatable mattress, while she had an old mat that barely separated her from the ground. "If you want, we can trade," I proposed, though I intuited that wasn't the issue.

"No," she said, with a shy, sad laugh. "It's not because of the mattress. Don't worry, it's nothing serious."

We were silent until my aunt shouted that lunch was ready. But it wasn't an uncomfortable silence. It was a silence that we shared, intimate and free of evasive looks—the kind of silence that comes after a secret is told.

"This year you apply yourself and get into a better school, one not too far from home, but better. Republica de Paraguay, maybe, they have English from kindergarten on . . . and maybe two years after that, in seventh grade, you change to any one of the emblematic schools, Lastarria, the National Institute . . . and from there straight to college." My aunt Veronica was arranging my future while we were walking back to the campground at night.

We were coming from the Suizo, a relic of an arcade that had pool tables, pinball machines, and video games, in a town two kilometers from the campground. All the patrons were old men. I didn't even glance at the video games, laughable beside my second-hand PlayStation—a birthday present from Mami. Instead, I asked my aunt to teach me to play pool.

She said she was good because her older brother had taught her when she was little. He'd had to babysit her, and since he didn't like to be in the house he took her with him to the pool hall. It was strange to imagine my aunt with a cue in hand. Pool seemed like a masculine game, one that called for patience and, because of its context, an element of vulgarity—characteristics completely alien to my aunt's personality. But there she was, carefully analyzing each shot, leaning far over the table, and when she made the first ball she winked at me and said with a smile: "Some things you never forget." In the end all four of us played, three women and a little boy, under the suspicious gazes of the rough men at the other tables. I couldn't have enjoyed myself more. Just as on days when we played rummy in the kitchen tent, the local radio station on in the background, I was flooded with a kind of satisfaction. I liked spending time with them, as one more member of their family.

"I spent a whole summer getting the girls ready for Carmela, didn't I?" my aunt went on proudly. "A summer just like this one. I wouldn't let them go swimming until they studied and did the day's exercises."

My aunt Veronica was really named Rosa, just like Mami. When I asked why she didn't use her first name, she told me she didn't like it, that it was an old lady's name, common and plain.

"What do you want to study, Nico?" asked Camila.

"Study?"

"Yeah, what do you want to be when you grow up? Lawyer, doctor, engineer, teacher . . ."

"Soccer player!"

"No, soccer players are dumb," said Camila.

"Then . . . soldier!"

"Soldier?" my aunt said in surprise. "Where'd you get that idea? Soldier . . . no, that's not a profession."

"In the commercials they parachute from planes," I said, running forward with my arms out like wings. Then I stopped in front of them, and imitating the intrepid voice in the commercial, I parroted: "You need more than good grades to get in."

"Those commercials are all lies," said Camila. "The military is bad. They brainwash the people who enlist." She took my head between her hands and started to shake it like a washing machine. "Don't you know what the military did in Chile?"

"No," I said, a little ashamed.

"They killed a lot of people. Under Pinochet's dictatorship. Do you know who Pinochet was, even?"

More shame, although the name sounded familiar.

"Then I'm going to be a detective," I said, and I looked at Javiera, expecting her to encourage me, but she was walking a little behind us and didn't look up from the ground.

"A rat? No, those are worse," said Camila. "More brainwashing." And she shook my head around again.

"You're intelligent, son," said my aunt. "You can't waste your potential like that. You have to study something, anything, but at university."

We were walking in the dark on one side of the road. If it hadn't been for the headlights of the cars that passed from time to time, and the stars, abundant and bright as I'd never seen in Santiago, we would hardly have seen the tips of our noses. A dark and silent night. Scary, when I thought about how we were unarmed. But I felt calm. I felt safe, and the word *safety* also sounded like something new to me. We'd been on vacation for a week and a half, and my wary attitude had started to soften. I was ceding. Suddenly I was letting myself be guided along, just like on that dark night, by the good wishes of my aunt and my cousins.

I couldn't waste my potential. My brother Mauri had wasted

his, but I couldn't. Almost everyone thought Mauri was some kind of Zé Pequeno. One aunt hid her purse when she went to my grandmother's house and he was there. It seemed to me a little extreme, because I knew my brother wasn't like that. I was only just starting to understand why he wasn't. Mauri wasn't even clever enough to be a criminal. I was five years younger, and I had to explain a lot of things to him. When he disappeared and didn't come home for several days, it was because he was keeping watch over cars; I'd gone with him myself a couple of times.

I was suddenly starting to understand many things. My father, for example. The matter was never discussed much, but I had always thought he was in prison for shoplifting. That was what my mother used to do, steal things from department stores and then sell them. Only a minor crime, petty and morally irreproachable, given the social injustices of the world. But then I realized that my mother wasn't in jail and he was, and that he'd been locked up for a little less than the time I'd been alive. No one goes to jail that long for shoplifting. What had he done? How had I not realized sooner?

I was ashamed to ask my aunt, not so much because my dad was in jail, but because of how naïve I'd been to not realize sooner that I didn't know why he was there. At the beach I didn't have anyone else to ask, and maybe it was better not to. But one day, I blurted it out.

My aunt was teaching me to float on my back. She told me the key was to keep my stomach out. She held my back for a while, and, just like when someone teaches you to ride a bike, she suddenly took her hands away without my realizing. She was the only one of the three who would go into the water with me. Javiera was very fussy and she barely got her feet wet.

"Why has my dad been in jail so many years?"

"Karen never told you?" asked my aunt, dubious. She was wearing a blue bathing suit with a gold belt around the waist.

"No."

"Why do you want to know now?"

I shrugged and went underwater for a second. When I came up, she moved closer to me and caressed my wet hair.

"I don't know much. But I think it's better for her to tell you. Are you sad that your dad is in jail?"

"No," I said naturally, and it was true. I sank down, leaving my eyes above water like a crocodile's.

"Well...In any case you don't have to worry. You're just beginning to live. You have all the opportunity in the world ahead of you. The important thing is that you know it's up to you to lead a good life. And that you're capable—"

"And I'm clever and smart," I said, interrupting her in a tone of false modesty, and then I burst out laughing.

"Yes, you're clever and smart. And you also have me and your grandmother."

I was capable. Suddenly, my aunt's rigor and aspirations didn't feel like the oppressive collar around a dog's neck. A master was also someone who petted and protected you. Her guidance started to hold something encouraging. Maybe it was true that my streets were full of danger. Maybe, if they were concerned about me, if they wanted to organize and improve my life, it was because they cared about me. Maybe I could be that polite, educated youth that they wanted for my future.

It was seductive to think of myself as a different person, and I was curious about all those things I was unfamiliar with. The habits. Brushing your teeth three times a day; bathing every night; blow-drying your hair; well-defined schedules for breakfast, lunch, and dinner; medicines for insect bites; lights out before midnight; clean clothes every morning. Most children find it boring and annoying to receive orders every second, but for me it was something unknown and original, something to value. It's not so easy to rebel when no one has ever put limits on you. Following instructions seemed like it would make things much simpler. And there was something tempting about it. It was tempting to imagine the prosperous life of a protected child.

Near the end of that vacation, I made a friend. The kind you make at the beach, whose name you've forgotten by May. Although I do remember his: Lucas.

His parents had a giant white house behind a dune, and they let him ride a four-wheeler on the campground beach. He must have been my age, though he looked a lot older. He was tall, fat, red-headed, and freckled. Maybe in reality he looked his age and I, short and skinny, was the one who looked younger. He was *cuico*, posh, the first *cuico* kid I ever met, and I taught him to ride waves and swim a few strokes, just like my aunt had taught me. I also taught him to snap his fingers—something Mauri had taught me—and, since he was afraid to go out very far, I told him how the deepest part of the ocean was in the Pacific, at 10,924 meters. When he asked me how I knew, I told him I'd read it in a book. I could not have been prouder. I could feel his admiration, and that he wanted me to tell him more things, and I started talking about Sherlock Holmes and Watson like it was no big deal, as If I'd been reading about them my whole life.

He followed me around for a couple of days, and while it wasn't especially fun to spend time with him, he let me ride the four-wheeler and even drive it. An orange Yamaha, I also remember that clearly. He tried to impress me by telling me how they'd brought it here from the United States, and I said, "What for? They sell four-wheelers here." He looked at me in astonishment.

My aunt let me play with the steering wheel and gear shift of her Kia, but that was nothing compared with driving the four-wheeler over the dunes. The feeling of being superior to Lucas in every regard was also incomparable: I was smarter, more agile, and braver. The only thing he beat me in was having money. But that aspect, the fact that I was poor and still better than him only increased my joy.

It happened one morning while Javiera was reading, leaning against the umbrella, and I was playing with Lucas in the water. I was teaching him to spit when my aunt appeared on the shore. She was wearing a wrap and a floppy sun hat.

"Nico, sunscreen!" she shouted, bottle in hand. Every morning before going shopping, she came into the tent and smeared me with sunscreen while I was still half asleep.

"I put it on myself," I lied, staying where I was.

"What about your back?"

"Javiera got it," I said.

"Okay. Lunch'll be ready in half an hour."

I asked what it was.

"Fish and french fries," she said, and smiled at me.

"Awesome!" I yelled, hitting the water, and I turned around to go on explaining to my friend how he had to hold his tongue to spit just right.

"You've got to like press it against your upper lip and—"

"Is that your mom? Man, she's pretty," he interrupted.

"Yeah," I answered. "She's pretty."

I looked at the immense ocean in front of me and I felt my knees go weak under the water. They were giving out, and for a second, in spite of the excellent swimmer I'd become in those days, I thought I could go under and drown right there.

"How old is she? She looks really young." He wasn't looking at me, he'd turned to watch my aunt walk away over the sand. I wanted to look at her too, but the only image that came to my mind was of my mother. My real mother, my ugly mama. I went under, and I realized my face was red because the water felt very cold. I swam to get away from Lucas, but he followed me.

"How old is she, man?" he asked me when I surfaced again.

I shrugged.

"You don't know how old your mom is?" he asked, surprised.

"Forty-five."

"I'm the runt of my family too . . . but my mom doesn't look so young, and she even uses a ton of lotions. How does yours do it?"

I cut him off: "She's just pretty, is all."

"Your sisters are pretty too."

"Yeah, yeah, yeah."

"But you don't look like them . . . Is your dad darker?"

He looked at my arms, even darker now from the summer sun. I don't think Lucas wanted to make me uncomfortable. He was honest, he was saying what he thought. Maybe, just as I'd never met a rich kid before, he'd never been around such a dark-skinned boy. His questions were sincere, they reflected what he didn't understand, or what didn't entirely fit together in his mind: children should look like their parents. But still, I *was* uncomfortable, and I wasn't going to let it go on.

"Is your dad the carrottop?"

"No, my mom," he replied. He sounded disconcerted, though not angry.

"Yeah, that's enough for today," I declared. "The waves are lame."

I quickly got out of the water, taking long strides against the current, overcoming it. I didn't say goodbye, and there were no plans to meet up again.

"Where's your friend?" Javiera asked when I went over to dry off.

"I got bored," I said. "He's so dumb . . ."

"It's just that no one is as brilliant as you, my dear Nicolai," she said, smiling, and she tickled my wet stomach.

"The only good thing he had was the four-wheeler," I confessed, and I felt a little lighter.

But then I saw my friend's orange head appear, and I felt a hammer come down on my chest. Lucas ambled over with a foolish and threatening smile.

"Hey, Nico," and he stopped to stand in front of us. "Ask your mom if you can come to my house today."

"Yeah, yeah, yeah," I replied. "Bye."

I started to nervously play with the sand. All my concentration on the sand, picking it up with one hand and letting it fall into the other. The sky was cloudy like every morning, but Javiera's eyes burned me like the desert sun. Lucas turned around, and after running off he shouted awkwardly:

"And tell her she's really pretty . . . and your sister, too."

We watched him run over the sand, trip, get up, and keep running toward his beach house. It was very funny to see the fat redhead fall, but there was no laughter. Javiera didn't say anything for a time that seemed endless to me. We looked out at the ocean, and I pretended nothing was happening. But I knew that Javiera had realized everything, and she knew it wasn't just a simple misunderstanding. It was also clear that she wouldn't ask me anything, much less scold me. She would keep to a perplexed silence, and that was even worse.

At a certain moment our eyes met. Mine distraught, hers intense. Behind that intensity I thought I saw disappointment, and beneath the disappointment something even worse: pity. Poor abandoned child, it's not his fault. My whole body tensed and I gave her a defiant look. I wasn't about to let people pity me, but then she smiled. "My Nicolai," she said, "my darling Nicolai . . ." and she lunged at me, pressing her whole weight on me, spreading her black hair that smelled like conditioner over my face to cover my eyes. And she planted kisses on my neck and head. "Nicolai . . . my dear Nicolai," she repeated, collapsing onto me again and again, like the languid heroines of the stories she was reading, and I played along, laughing and tickling her to get her off me.

After eating the lunch of fish and french fries that my aunt had made, I still felt strange. That first feeling of guilt can be a very bitter experience for children. In my case it wasn't the first time I had lied, but this wasn't just a simple deception, this was betrayal. I had denied my own mother. And what was even worse, I realized that over recent days I'd forgotten her completely, wishing, perhaps, that she was someone else.

That night, we didn't read. I crawled into my sleeping bag and covered myself completely. I thought about Mama. I wondered how she was, and I imagined her in the apartment in the dark, lying beside Mauri, killing time before going to sleep, with the same unconcerned expression as always, but getting old. And I missed her and was sorry for hurting her, even though she didn't know, and I was also sorry that because she didn't know, I had no way to apologize to her.

I felt disgusted with myself and I spent the whole night with my stomach in knots, thinking that the image of my mother would claw at me forever. By the next day I felt better. I guess it was the normalcy of things. Routine soothes any pain. You make mistakes and life goes on. I think it's a lesson that has to do with growing older. I was only ten years old, but I realized how everything in me quieted. Nothing was so serious.

There weren't many days left at the campground, and during the ones that followed I made an effort to keep acting the same with my cousins and my aunt. I showed myself willing to give and to achieve what they expected of me. I repeated the lesson like a good boy, but this time I knew very clearly that I was faking. On the last night we had a rummy championship, which I won, and the next morning we took down the tents, piled into the car, and headed back.

There was an accident waiting for us in Santiago. One night while Mauri was watching the cars, someone had driven over his foot. It happened in the middle of our vacation and they hadn't wanted to worry us. My brother couldn't tolerate the recommended bed rest, and it wasn't long before he sawed off his own cast. Both of us, Mauri with his limping foot and me with my new books under my arm, went back to my mother, and everything followed its normal course until my brother was stabbed in his crushed foot.

When Mauri went back to guarding cars, he found someone else had taken his place. And so as to leave no doubt that the spot no longer belonged to Mauri, the new guy stuck a knife in my brother's heel. He spent a few days in the hospital, but then he skipped out, and we didn't see him again until he turned up in San José Hospital, where they amputated his foot.

That event was an inflection point for my grandmother, and with my aunt Veronica's help she started the process of filing a complaint against my mother in family court. She wanted to get custody. Of me, not of Mauri, who they already considered a lost cause. With my mother's extensive record, it wouldn't take long for me to be placed in my grandmother's care. My aunt committed to helping her financially.

My grandmother explained her plans with a care and tenderness I'd never known in her, but I replied violently that if she separated me from my mother, if she forced me to live with her and my grandfather, I was going to run away, I'd run away just like Mauri. I'd leave a thousand times if I had to.

My grandmother knew I had her between a rock and a hard place. If she reported me for running away, the police would put me in a group home; that was what the law stipulated if the new guardian was unable to take responsibility. And she also knew that being sent to a group home was an even worse fate than staying with my mom. So the whole thing went nowhere and I kept living more or less as before, except that for Christmas I received two new gifts: clothes from my aunt and a book from Javiera.

A girlfriend I had a long time ago told me that when she was six years old, her mother had asked her: "Do you want me to leave your father?" She used to cry and suffer with her parents' bitter, daily fights, but when her mother asked that question, an immediate and categorical no emerged from her mouth. Things got worse and after a few years her father left them, and they started having a ton of financial problems and heartaches. My girlfriend told me that during much of her childhood, and even after she grew up, she'd wondered what would have happened if she had answered yes. Maybe they would have saved themselves a lot of sorrow. She tended to feel unsatisfied with her life and she thought that if things had been different, "better," she wouldn't have to carry around all those insecurities that made her so unhappy. I told her that she was a twenty-five-year-old woman and she couldn't go around holding her parents responsible for her life; she had to learn to accept things, that everybody makes do with what they have. I felt like I was talking to a little girl, and I told her how childish she was.

I used to say that kind of thing to people, with a lilt of unbreakable self-confidence. But the truth is, the memory of that summer I spent with my aunt and my cousins tends to come back to my mind every once in a while, just as my ex-girlfriend's memories revisited her.

Returning to my childhood. When I slept at my grandmother's house, she would wake me up, give me breakfast, and take me to school. And if I spent the night in the apartment in the projects, she called my mother's cell phone at seven in the morning to wake me up. I think about my aunt's intentions. She wanted to help me, show me another reality, get me out of the projects, get me to college. To her, that meant being a better person. But I refused that future of well-being, and, as she put it back then, I wasted my potential. I didn't study anything in college and I ended up as not much more than what my parents were. I didn't want to disappoint her, not her or my grandmother or myself, but accepting the hand they were holding out to me meant stripping myself of many things. It meant sloughing off who I was then. And who was I? I was a boy who loved his mother above all things, and I was going to stay with her, I wasn't going to betray her again. I guess I knew that maybe my mother wasn't the prettiest, and it wasn't likely she'd ever take me on vacation or make me the food I liked, but she was my mother, and if I wasn't by her side, no one else was going to love her.

For a time I'd thought that if I separated from my mother I would get caught up in one lie after another and live another person's story, one that didn't correspond to me. Wasting my potential, resigning myself to my life, was the only way I saw to be honest. But the truth is—and maybe this is why I can't forget those days in La Serena—that once I was back with my mother and my brother, I wasn't the same as before. A part of me was lost forever and I was caught between two selves, the one I was and the one I could have been. Although I try, I can barely reconstruct the voice of that ten-year-old boy, before that vacation—the last vacation he'd ever have.

Maybe it seems exaggerated to spend so much time going back over such a small thing, just as it's exaggerated to think that such a young boy can really make a decision that will determine his life.

It's exaggerated to talk about honesty, when I got myself into plenty of problems as a teenager, particularly after my father got out of jail. But all I can do is hold on to all those exaggerations, and believe in them. Believe, like my cousin Javiera, that every detail means something. All I can do is to try to fit—or force—each piece into place, so everything achieves its meaning. Maybe I'm just an overly concrete person, one who can't manage in the world without possessing a few key certainties.

During the years that came later, I faced problems much more dramatic than the ones I experienced at ten years old. But staying with my mother, taking care of her as best I could, became a kind of consolation. Just as it was a consolation to go on reading and to convince myself that, when the moment came, I would be as prepared as possible to face the circumstances.

Lucky Me

When Denise dropped the mirror and it hit the floor, the upstairs neighbor stopped her moaning. The glass cracked a little at the edge and the noise was minimal, almost imperceptible, one more among the many little explosions so routine in an ordinary apartment building like this one. But the neighbor knew exactly where the sound was coming from and she stopped moaning, though she didn't stop moving. It was a mental distraction, not a physical one.

Denise, hidden on the other side of the door, remained alert. She was sitting cross-legged in the hallway of her rented apartment. The hallway that joined the two bedrooms and separated them from the living room. A hallway that was redundant in contemporary buildings. A hallway from an age when hallways were needed to shield the bedrooms. An age when there were more hallways than rooms. Without the mirror she'd been holding and using as a viewfinder—focusing it like a camera to get a good view of the scene in her bedroom—she had to settle for hearing the sound of the bodies. A less intense sound than the moans of desire and pain she'd heard in the past. Their movements were muffled by clothes, and the sound was the friction of cloth rather than the watery slap she usually associated with sex. Because the couple never got completely naked, though not out of shame or modesty. They left their clothes on because for them it was necessary. Denise had come to understand that. They seemed to enjoy imposing limits and obstacles on themselves. They liked not being entirely accessible to each other, liked to take detours. The times when she had perceived them to experience the most pleasure was when Juan Carlos penetrated the woman with her underwear still on. He'd move the lower part aside, keep his fingers there, and their breathing would grow agitated.

Denise closed her eyes. She rested the palm of her hand on the cold floor, waiting for what she knew would come next. The neighbor moaned again. But this moan was different from the one a few minutes before; Denise had learned to differentiate and interpret. She was sure that this specific moan was a signal for a pattern that would follow: the woman would take the bottom position so Juan Carlos's back would be turned toward the door and Denise and there was no danger he'd see her—though in any case, he wasn't likely to get distracted from what he was doing. Then the volume and speed of their rhythmic plaint would build until the woman displayed her climax with a spate of little cries, which he would follow, reaching his own orgasm with a combination of snorting, moaning, and cursing. Denise wouldn't be able to see it, but she was sure Juan Carlos would grab hold of the pillows, stifling his cries as he covered his face, and that the upstairs neighbor would have her eyes tightly shut, as if she were driving a car straight into a wall.

The moan foretold all this and so it went, and it all lasted a couple of minutes. Afterward, Denise's apartment was silent again, a silence of everyday noises. Denise thought, as she had other times on witnessing this kind of ending, that among all the disadvantages of being a woman, this was one of the worst: faking. Women had the power to fake it.

The epilogue tended to be characterized by the woman's withdrawal and the man's need for closeness; he held her neck and caressed her nipples as if he were trying to calm her that way, as if he were spreading Mentholatum on a congested chest. But Denise didn't stick around for that this time; there wasn't much to hear.

She got to her feet without picking up the cracked mirror from the floor. It didn't matter if she left it lying there, the woman would soon return it to her. Denise knew her neighbor would knock on the door of the other bedroom, where Denise was retreating, and she would have the mirror in her hands. Because the neighbor had realized a long time ago, she'd known almost since the beginning, since the first time their eyes met in the reflection. There'd been a fingerprint on the glass, and on that spot of dried sweat, Denise had looked into her neighbor's eyes. They shone, they held surprise but not anger. Denise had returned the gaze, in the mirror, on the fingerprint. And her eyes had been apologetic and defensive at the same time.

She tiptoed away into the room next door—the French girl's room. She turned the doorknob slowly, silently, then went in and sat down on the bed.

After a while it came as she'd imagined: the knock on the door.

A soft knock. Denise got up to answer, still on tiptoe. There was the neighbor, her eyes fixed on the floor. Denise moved aside and the woman hunched over a little as she came in, as if she were entering a low tunnel or making a kind of bow. She had the mirror in her hands, and she walked over to the bed and stood there wearing her patient expression. She handed Denise the mirror with its cracked edge, and Denise took it and put it facedown on the bed, the reflection turned to pure darkness.

"We're not going to come anymore," said the neighbor lady in her usual diffident voice.

"Yes," said Denise, "I understand."

They looked each other in the eyes, just as they had on other occasions, in the mirror.

"I still haven't told Juan Carlos," the upstairs neighbor continued. "That we're not going to come to your apartment anymore and that . . ." She stopped speaking. She shook her head, as if confused by her own words. She seemed more unsure than usual. "I mean . . . What I mean is . . ." she stuttered. "We're not going to come, and Juan Carlos doesn't know anything. Neither thing, and Juan Carlos, Juan Carlos . . ."

She didn't go on explaining, it wasn't necessary. Denise understood, and the neighbor lady was finally sure of something too. She had made a decision, and the name Juan Carlos, the man's name, went on resonating above them, imposing itself on them, contaminating them like smog, aiding them like a reference point on a map, consuming and caressing them at once, like love.

✦

The first time Carolina talked to me, we were walking home from school down Berna. I was flipping through my *Sailor Moon* album, so spellbound I was incapable of watching where I was going, and every once in a while I tripped. Beyond my fanaticism for the cartoons, my delight was heightened by the fact that my mother had forbidden me to spend money on stickers. I collected them in secret, and in a couple of blocks, when I got home, I would have to hide the album in the neighbor's privet hedge.

"You like *Sailor Moon*?" I heard a voice say beside me, and I started in surprise and slammed the album shut.

"Which one are you?" the voice spoke again.

I squinted at her: a girl I didn't know, but whose sweater bore the same insignia as mine.

"Mercury," I replied, hesitant. Mercury was the character I told other people I was. I chose the silent, studious teenager with short hair, even though deep down I longed for the starring role of Serena, all high ponytails and spontaneity.

"I'm Pluto," said Carolina.

I nodded, trying to hide the fact that I didn't know the character, but fully aware that my unenthusiastic expression gave away the terrible fact that I didn't have cable, that I was doomed to spending afternoons watching reruns of *El Club de los Tigritos*.

"She's in 'Sailor Moon S,' along with Sailor Uranus and Sailor Neptune," she clarified. "How many are you missing?"

"Eight," I said proudly, to redeem myself for my ignorance.

"You have to buy them outside of Salo," Carolina advised with a knowing air, seemingly unimpressed by the number. "There are guys who sell them for fifty pesos . . . a hundred for the hardest ones. I'm missing a lot, but it's because I also collect *Saint Seiya*. Do you like *The Knights of the Zodiac*? I like them a lot more than *Sailor Moon*."

Again, I didn't know what to say. *The Knights of the Zodiac* . . . I didn't watch them much. They attracted me, yes, but in a way I didn't understand well, not like my innate adoration for *Sailor Moon*. I drew a blank, and now I couldn't even nod to hide my lack of knowledge. I'd been exposed: I didn't know. Perplexed in front of Carolina, I felt panic. It was a feeling I was to experience often, every time a chasm opened up between me—a little girl—and an opinion—something to hold on to. Carolina, with her judgments of the world around her, seemed to have no problems there.

"Want to come watch it at my house?" she asked.

I nodded again. And then, as would also happen so many times in the future, the panic became pleasant, attractive. A hand appeared on the scene, and whether it was reaching out to support me like a bridge or to shove me from behind, it would force me across that chasm.

I put the album under my arm and followed her down Berna. While we walked, I looked at her more closely. She was very thin and had long legs and arms covered with a lot of dark hair. Judging by her height, she had to be a couple of years above me. She wore a white headband and had her hair pulled back in a bun so thick I guessed it must reach below her waist when it was loose. I was impressed by long hair then because I supposed that feminine beauty resided there, or at least that's what I'd heard a boy in my class say once: the prettiest ones are the ones with the longest hair. I wore my own

hair in a very short bob, shorn on the neck. My dad took me to the
hairdresser and chose the cut: the easiest to style in the mornings.
He said I was pretty enough as I was, and anything more was just
vanity. My dad had a broken nose and several false teeth, so he must
have known a thing or two about vanity. It's not that I thought what
my classmate said was true; in fact, when I'd heard his comment,
I realized for the first time how stupid boys—and men—can be.
But after so many years of that pruned style, I pined for the long,
flowing hair of a mermaid.

During those first minutes together I couldn't decide if Carolina was pretty or not. What I did know was that she stood out, and
that she didn't seem to care much about her appearance. Her knees
were covered in scars. I had a few too, and they made me feel ugly
and unfeminine, but she seemed to display hers proudly, like battle
scars, symbols of life well lived. She was different from me—I realized that right away. Different from my short hair and extra kilos,
my yellow skin and my round and guileless face.

When we reached Tokio we turned right. My house was to the
left, and when I found myself turning the other way I was filled
with satisfaction. I was breaking the rules again. I was always on
the lookout for the forbidden, though in the innocuous manner
of a sheltered child. Stealing a Negrita candy bar in the supermarket, collecting stickers in secret, going somewhere else before
I went home. Without permission, without letting anyone know.
It seemed like the only way to get a taste of that real world my
parents protected me from. Even if no one else knew. Even if my
classmates felt sorry for me for being a sheltered little girl. Being
overprotected was one of the most terrible humiliations that existed, and that's why I isolated myself. I tried to go unnoticed and

I sidestepped friendships. It was better not to have friends than to endure mockery and pity.

I walked happily beside Carolina down the streets of Conchalí. Not even when we crossed Cardenal Caro and my house was left far behind, or when I saw some men drinking on the corner, or when the buildings started to look too poor—not even then did the joy in my heart diminish. I was walking freely, or at least unconcernedly—the closest I got to freedom, on occasion.

Carolina waved at an old man who was sweeping dry leaves in the street; he barely looked up from his task. Her house, situated on a corner, was one story and very large. The porch went all the way along it, with an arbor lending it shade. She opened the gate, and two large dogs came running over. She told me they were harmless, and she went to the end of the porch where an old lady was sitting on a four-person sofa; Carolina greeted her with a "Hi, Grandma." The grandmother's hands rested on her lap and she was looking ahead in a contemplative pose, so serene that it seemed she'd spent a long time in that same position, like the Buddhas my dad had told me about.

"Your granddad's going to eat at two, you want to eat with him?" the grandmother asked. "Hello, dear," she added when she saw me dodging the dogs' snouts as they sniffed me.

"I'll see later," replied Carolina.

"I'll see later," repeated the grandmother, winking an eye. "This one always just sees later," she said, shaking her head, her eyes laughing.

"We'll be in my room," said Carolina, and she went inside.

"Okay, okay," said the grandmother, and her gaze returned to the horizon.

"This is my bed, and this is my mom's," said Carolina, pointing to the twin beds in the room off the end of the porch. The place was built of wood and seemed a little tilted. The floorboards creaked, and it smelled like a hair salon. "This one's for my brother when he sleeps here, but sometimes an uncle uses it too."

I had a brother too, but I didn't see him much and I didn't mention him to Carolina. "Half brother, on my dad's side," was how I always clarified things if the subject came up, just as my mother had taught me.

Carolina took three albums out of a wicker stand, sat on the rug, and opened the *Sailor* one on her crossed legs.

"You have your stickers?"

Still standing up, I had noticed the dressing table in the opposite corner. It was white with an oval mirror, and it was overflowing with jars of lotion, perfume bottles, and little boxes stuffed with necklaces. On a bench to the right was an apparatus for hardwax hair removal, and on the floor, a pile of magazines. Around the mirror there were cutout pictures of women wearing hats and party dresses. The only one I recognized was Lady Di.

"My mom is crazy about the monarchy. That's why she named me Carolina," said Carolina. "Speaking of which, what's your name?"

"Nicole," I said. "Nicole de la Cruz."

"Nicole," she repeated, weighing the name. "It's with an *e* at the end, right?"

I nodded.

"I like it," she decided. "It ends with a strong syllable. I'm Carolina, for Caroline of Monaco. But I don't like it because it ends in *ina*, which sounds little and sweet. So you can just call me Caro."

My name. Nicole. I was glad it wasn't Camila, like six of my classmates, but I'd always thought it was too masculine because it didn't have any *a*'s, and it ended in *e*. I liked that Carolina—Caro—liked it.

"You're in fourth grade, right? I remember you. Last year you got the award for best student, right?" I nodded, a little ashamed. "I'm in fifth grade," she said.

She told me that when she was in fourth grade she had fought for the religion award. She didn't really know why she wanted it, but she'd made every effort to make it hers. She helped the teacher with whatever she needed, led morning prayer, read the Old Testament stories, and participated in all the class discussions. She had even come to deny the existence of dinosaurs, jumping all over her classmates who were fans of *Jurassic Park* and berating the pseudo-paleontologists who collected little plastic bones. She'd been sure that certificate would have her name on it, but in the end-of-year ceremony they called another student up. He was Catholic, yes, but he never said a word, Caro told me, he didn't even know the Creed or the other, lesser-known prayers. It hurt her that they chose him and she felt it was a betrayal, so the next year she didn't even look at the teacher, and she also gave up religion. Then it happened that she started getting on the good side of the Philosophy for Children teacher. She didn't try, she just said whatever came into her head without thinking about it much—random things, like how Santa Claus's suit is red because of Coca-Cola—but the comments seemed to please the teacher. In the end he gave her the award for best student. She'd hung it over her bed for a while, but then she took it down; she'd realized that awards didn't matter.

I listened to her, impressed, and when she finished I gathered my courage and told her that my dad always said the Old Testament was a metaphor. I didn't really understand what a metaphor was, but Caro nodded and said my father was an intelligent man.

We traded stickers. Caro didn't have any that I needed, but I agreed to give her whichever ones she was missing. We traded a lot of our doubles, and we played hand-clapping games for them. Then Caro took another album from the wicker stand. "The most precious," she said with a sly smile. It was a real album, for photos, with thick cardboard pages and plastic protectors. It contained a series of black-and-white images, clippings from encyclopedia articles, and drawings Caro had done herself.

Pompeii. She said she'd been obsessed with the Pompeii ruins ever since she saw a documentary about them on the National Geographic channel. She told me about Mount Vesuvius's violent and mysterious eruption on August 24 in A.D. 79. I noticed that when she spoke she changed some *s*'s for *f*'s, but her voice was no less captivating for that, emphatic and serene at the same time. She described the Garden of Fugitives and the horrific statues that the archaeologist Giuseppe Fiorelli molded from the hollows left by the citizens buried in lava. Never before had I paid such close attention to anyone. Her words shone, they gave off power, and I listened to her as if she were dictating instructions on how to live my own life. Again, Caro overwhelmed me with all those things I didn't know, but I was willing to learn and to feel just the way she did. We went to the kitchen and she made tomato-and-cheese sandwiches in the microwave. A microwave! Another thing we didn't have at

my house—in addition to Caro's giant cable TV, much bigger than
the 14-inch set in my living room—and it astonished me again.
Caro drank water straight from the tap and then offered to let me
drink. Though I was thirsty I held back, as I always did in such situations, because meningitis was going around and it was dangerous
to share saliva. Of course, later that same day, when we bought
Popsicles at a neighbor's house and Caro offered to exchange fla-
vors, I forgot about meningitis and sucked on her saliva fearlessly.
That afternoon we walked to the water tower and stared up at it as
if it were a monument. We wandered independently, from Juanita
Aguirre to El Cortijo. No adult interfered in what we said or did,
and we didn't mention school or parents again, because it almost
seemed like they didn't exist, as if we really were the masters of
our decisions and had time and food at our disposal, and we could
leave any impediment—study and family—behind. There was a
commercial for a new *Sailor Moon* album and we cheered, but then
Caro admitted that her allowance wasn't big enough for her to collect another album. I didn't even have permission, but I didn't dare
admit that, and I proposed, strategically, that we join forces. We
agreed to collect it together, our first pact as friends.

At five, *Saint Seiya: Knights of the Zodiac* came on the ETC channel. We sat on the rug very close to the TV, the volume turned up
as high as it would go, and Caro recited the opening without missing a line: "Legend tells us the knights will appear every time the
world falls into the hands of the forces of evil." I had a sensation of
pleasure and relief, similar to the one I felt when I sat on the corner
by my school building to let the wind swirl around my back and
tickle me. A feeling that combined somnolence and solemnity, and
that I wished would never end . . . And no one will ever be able to

define the happiness of sitting on the rug and watching *Knights of the Zodiac* one day after school, without parents, a tomato-and-cheese sandwich in my hands.

✦

Denise trudged up the stairs: head bowed, hand clinging to the concrete ledge to haul herself onward. A sigh every three steps, she was coming home. It was Friday, past eight in the evening. She was returning from the library, where she'd worked the front desk for the past three years. Exhausted, even though she'd stood up from her chair only a couple of times during her nine-hour shift.

When she'd applied for the job she was sure it was perfect for her: silence, dust, and books. She almost imagined herself as the heroine of a romantic novel, wandering among the shelves, surrounded by stories and trailing ethereal fingers over the spines of the books. Reality was considerably different. The library was in a mall, and it had mall schedules, mall patrons, and the fluorescent lights of a mall. The dust from the books made the skin on her hands split open. The dust and the alcohol gel, because every time she picked up a children's book with a sticky plastic cover, she squeezed out a couple of drops of hand sanitizer. She had read on a forum that libraries had twenty-eight times more bacteria and viruses than public bathrooms, and it was recommended to put library books into the microwave for a few seconds before starting to read them. It's not that she was obsessed with cleanliness—in her bedroom the coffee spoons accumulated one after the other on the nightstand, opaque like an antique collection, and she took out the garbage only when it couldn't hold one tea bag more. But that was the thing about a 45-hour-a-week job: everything ended up becoming a phobia.

For a time she'd paid special attention to the patrons, to what they read in the reading room and what they checked out, and she'd kept a list of strange readers.

Woman, 27, three books: *Biography of Father Hurtado*; *Biography of Saint Francis of Assisi*; *History of the Necronomicon*, by Lovecraft.

Man, 48, book and magazine: *Mysteries of Masonry*; January's *Cosmopolitan*.

Man, around 50 (always wears the same baseball cap, gray jacket, and navy-blue pants. Always!): photocopies a page about the parts of a cell from a children's encyclopedia.

The list had been dormant for a while. She spent the afternoons suffering from the heat, fanning herself with magazines—the air-conditioning had been broken since the day it was installed. From time to time she wrinkled her nose in disgust at the food-court smells that inundated the library and mingled with its smell of confinement, of readers' breath and sticky books . . . She never wandered among the shelves with a bucolic expression, waiting for some title to surprise her. She spent most of the time—as much as she could—sitting at the computer reading articles on Pajama Surf and Rusofilia, the blog of a punk makeup artist and her Brooklynite boyfriend, all kinds of Tumblrs, forums about bacteria and viruses, Facebook. Bored. Avoiding greetings, replying in monosyllables, and hating anyone who asked her for a photocopy. She found getting up from her chair and going to war with a decrepit machine almost offensive, and all for a fifty-peso photocopy—which in itself was a scam. That's what it cost to get her to stand up: fifty pesos.

When she reached the third floor she let out one long, final

sigh. Her building was a cement cube of four floors. It was surrounded by a network of similar blocks connected by walkways and
parks with thick-trunked trees and high branches where various
species of birds nested. A good place to live, it had to be said. After
four years there, Denise was still surprised when the noise of the
lawn mowers woke her up on Sundays. She had never lived with
the color green so close before, or such concern over gardens and
flowers. She'd spent most of her life in places where it was common
to pay the neighborhood drunk a few coins to pull up the weeds. In
her first years, she was caught up in the novelty of Ñuñoa, and she
used to go out with her camera to walk around the neighborhood
plazas and through Park Juan XXIII. She crossed the strap of her
compact Fujifilm camera over her body as if she were carrying a
revolver under her arm, and she wore a gray sweatshirt, her cam-
ouflage uniform. She liked to get lost in those streets, so different
from hers, and look at the old mansions, with their modernist ar-
chitecture from the '50s, many of them empty or converted into
homes for the elderly, or marketing headquarters teeming with
pretty promoters. She would put her head through the bars and
take photos of the well-tended lawns, the dry branches held like
captive snakes in metal bars, the half-open window of an abandoned
house, university students who went by looking very serious or very
happy, the promoters smoking and talking while they hastily applied makeup. The old people in the homes were her best subjects,
or at least the ones who most enjoyed having their picture taken.
They posed smiling, or stared at the purple flowers that fell from
the jacarandas while they waited for the day to end. She knew that
one of the advantages of being a woman was that she came off as
less threatening, but in any case she tried to go unnoticed when

she took a picture, which was why she had chosen a small camera. Except with the old folks, whom she always greeted and thanked afterward. They often invited her inside, and on one occasion, in spite of her uneasiness, in spite of her idea that the photographer was an observer and not a participant and should maintain distance, she went farther in than usual and took one of her favorite photos: a close-up of a ninety-one-year-old woman who was smoking, half hidden in the backyard, her face mischievous, full, lucid.

That time was gone, and now she walked without noticing anyone, tired steps in a straight line from work to home, sighs between landings, spoons accumulating on the nightstand, leaving the apartment only when one more tea bag wouldn't fit and she had to take out the trash.

Her neighbor from across the way, the one who collected the condominium fees, was smoking in the open hallway the residents shared. She must have been over fifty, and nearly every night, more or less at the same time, she came outside to smoke and flaunt her round little body and her badly dyed blond hair. She greeted Denise and asked a couple of questions that Denise dodged with a "Good, all good" and an overwhelmed expression. She distrusted that friendliness, and she wondered with a certain irritation if the woman didn't have anything better to do. To Denise, the condo-fee neighbor was just an old woman who went outside right at the hour when almost everyone was coming home from work, just to spy and gossip about every insignificant thing that went on in the building.

———

She made an instant coffee and went to her room. Tossed her back-pack on the bed, turned on the computer. She sat down at the desk. Stood up again and almost knocked over a mug holding leftover coffee and paper shreds. She was an expert in accumulating paper—old Post-its, receipts, tickets, metro balances—which she tore into even smaller pieces and left scattered everywhere. In her room, every movement implied danger. The chair's wheels got caught up in the sneakers, the clothes thrown on the floor, the socks and bras, the PC cables, the phone charger, the extension cord, the cords of the speakers and the lamp. She was constantly tripping over things and ended up practically imprisoned, sunk in the quicksand of her room.

She went to the French girl's room and sat on her double bed. Soon after she'd moved in, the French girl had commented on how strange she found it that Denise slept on a twin bed; apparently in France only children had single mattresses. Denise observed the room with her coffee in hand. The smell was very different from the one in her own room. It was a terribly pleasant and feminine smell, reeking of Lush soaps and perfumes and the L'Occitane lotions that the girl's mother sent from France. Denise had been living with the French girl for six months, and she often snuck into her room when she was out. She liked to inhabit this foreign space. Nose around here and there, rifle through the souvenirs from the girl's travels, hold them in her hands: a little Mapuche doll, postcards, photos with friends, little wooden boxes holding copper earrings, bitter chocolates, and gourmet jams. From each object rose an affirmation of her self: this was hers and she was proud, and Denise wanted to feel part of that even if it was only for a few minutes, just like when she used to walk through the Ñuñoa streets.

The French girl. Her name was Josiane, she was tall and solid, overgrown. She was studying for a postgraduate degree in Latin American studies, and she wore three woven bracelets tied around her wrist: one was a gift from her best French friend, Kallisté; another, from her best friend in Brazil, Paulo; the third, from her best friend in Barcelona, Lupi. Denise smoothed the alpaca wool blanket that covered the bed and looked at her bare arm, which wore not a single bracelet. Before she'd left on her trip to Machu Picchu, Bolivia, and Ecuador, the French girl had warned Denise that she hoped things between them would improve when she got back, and if not, she would look for another place. Denise didn't understand what she meant; she didn't think there was any problem with their living situation. In her nearly perfect Spanish, the French girl had explained that what she wanted was for them to have more of a relationship, to talk, spend time together, drinking tea and listening to music in the living room, for example. That was why she traveled, she said, to get to know people, to gain experience. Denise had looked at her with the same overwhelmed expression she gave the condo-fee neighbor. "You don't gain experience," she told the French girl, "you accumulate encounters, because all you do is have a good time. Experience makes you suffer."

The French girl stared at her openmouthed. "See," she scolded. "That's exactly what I'm talking about."

It's not that she didn't like Josiane, but she couldn't respect her. She couldn't respect any European, the same way she couldn't respect the sufferings of rich people. That's why she always said no when Josiane invited her to go out with her foreign friends. But she did like to be in the French girl's room, among her things. Once, she'd even picked up her Nikon, expensive and much better than her own camera, and she'd taken a couple photos of the hallway. It was dusk, and the sun imprinted reddish tones on the wall that mixed with the shadows of the apartment. She'd forgotten to erase the last one, and sometime later the French girl had put the photo on Facebook, amazed by what she thought was a paranormal event. No, Denise couldn't respect her.

Of course, there was something of envy there. She envied Josiane's assuredness, her stride of a European conqueror, her ability to take ownership of the places she inhabited. Denise had spent her childhood in Santiago, her adolescence in Vallenar, and her early adulthood in Antofagasta, and she'd never felt she belonged anywhere. She had followed her mother's nomadic roaming, and as she was living in shared rooms in other people's houses, the hope began gestating that when she finally found herself surrounded by her own things, she would feel something in her heart. She'd returned to Santiago to study photography in an institute, and she had decorated her rented room enthusiastically, meticulously. She painted one wall burgundy, went to the market and collected fruit boxes to make shelves, hung photographs by Robert Frank, Eudora Welty, Jill Freedman, and Sergio Larraín, and she even included some of her own in the mix; she made collages; bought an old wooden desk; went to Casa & Ideas for white candles, a mug with a little bird inside it, and a round paper lampshade . . . and then, when the room was finally full, she sat on the bed, closed her eyes, and practically cringed, as if she were waiting for a roller coaster to start its descent. But she didn't feel anything; she was still a tourist.

The closest she had gotten to the feeling she yearned for—indefinable even for her—was when she used to get off her night shift as a cook in a restaurant on Suecia. At around one thirty in the morning, a line of people would grow at the bus stop, almost all of them workers in Providencia like her. They waited in silence, and in the air you could feel the exhaustion and anxiety and also a certain defensiveness, and ten minutes or an hour could go by and everyone stayed just like that. Until the Transantiago buses appeared, three or four in a row, barreling in from far away, enormous, their lights up high, full of hope, like trucks carrying food to a village isolated by disaster. And as they approached, the workers' attitude changed and an energy started to course through them. Denise felt it too, and it was as though something were set free, as if they all let out a big sigh. The wait was over. In those seconds, on tiptoe with her head held high, she really did belong to a place, even if the place was also difficult to define, even if it didn't exist physically, because it wasn't the bus stop, or Transantiago, or the street. It was a place she could never stay.

No one visited her and she didn't bother to invite anyone over, and so it didn't even make superficial sense to worry about her room. No, putting down roots was definitely not for her, and when she realized that, she got rid of the decorations, sold her camera, and dropped out of her photography studies—the second major she had quit. She erased the files of her favorite photos: the blind man walking and holding a little boy's hand, the university student biting a Latin dictionary while he held a hot dog in his hands, the student protestor wearing a black ski mask with fox ears while he lit a barricade of tires on fire . . . At the end of the day, it wasn't that she aspired to take photographs for *National Geographic* or Magnum;

photography had just been an excuse to go back to Santiago and test those dreams that had gotten stuck in her head.

✦

Mesh netting hung from the roof of my parents' room on the second floor down to the kitchen on the first. My father had installed it so the sun wouldn't beat in so hard in the mornings. He slept in until after twelve because he worked nights at the airport. He tried to keep the room as dark as possible, the curtains drawn and the door closed, accumulating a warm torpor in the room that I liked because I related it to his personality during the first hours of his day, when he was sleepy and affectionate.

When I got home from school I'd press my ear to his door and try to figure out what was happening from the sounds I heard. On the other side I would hear "Om," and deep inhaling and exhaling. When I slipped in to greet him, the mats and blankets he used were still spread out on the floor. My mom said my father needed to meditate, and though I didn't really know what yoga was, I understood what she meant, since I knew his mood swings as well as she did. Hours before he left for work, he turned into another person. He went mute just before starting his shaving routine, and while he waited for the water to boil he paced around the house with his hands on his hips, taking furious steps. He took off his pajamas and tied a towel around his waist. He poured the water into the sink and submerged some washcloths that he pressed against his face. Then he let out some short wheezing sounds, like he was threatening to bellow. My father had sensitive skin, and it was a sacrifice for him to shave every day. To round off the ritual, he went out on the stairs and applied cologne while he cursed and grunted. After that you couldn't talk to him; just like his skin after shaving, everything irritated him. But at the same time you had to be attentive to him, observe his anger without expressing an opinion. If we were unconcerned by his hardship, that bothered him too.

If there was one thing I knew about my father, it was that he hated his job. The two Sundays and the Tuesday he had off every month were even worse for him. He was exhausted by the mere knowledge that he would have to go back to work the next day, and he couldn't rest. He spent the whole day aggrieved by the injustice of another workday, suffering the brevity of time and its implacable advance.

That's why I was so scared as I walked beside Caro's mom when she took me home that first day. It was my father's day off, and he had no qualms about offending people. I'd seen him complain and upset my teachers, phone operators, waiters, and salespeople, and then brag about it after he'd gotten a discount or a free dessert. I imagined the situation: my father would ask who had taken care of me all afternoon, and then make sarcastic remarks about all the supervision we'd surely gotten from a couple of old people. I saw him throwing it in Caro's mom's face that she was separated or a single mom, or that she didn't have her own house. With his hands on his hips, an ironic half smile on his face, chin raised. I also imagined my mother behind him, half hidden and silent. Forcing a scowl of anger to support her husband while she apologized with her eyes, those martyred eyes she used every time she said, "You know how your father is," or "What can *I* do?"

To me, my mother's passivity was even more unforgivable than my father's outbursts. Really, I forgave him for everything and loved him all the more. Because my father was also that other person, the one you could play dominoes and blackjack with. The one who took me to swim class on Saturday mornings and watched me the whole hour from the little window that looked over the heated pool at the YMCA. My father was the one who went with me to the swings at the playground, and on long bike rides from one neighborhood to another. He was the one who read me strange stories from the religion he practiced. The one who challenged me to figure out the combination to his briefcase in exchange for something of his that I wanted to use for a while, like a tool or a funny tie printed with a Bugs Bunny pattern. With orange-chirimoya ice cream in hand, we could take walks through the streets while he talked to me about subjects that I considered deep and interesting, like how "learning to breathe is learning to live . . ." My father was the one who, unlike my mother, took me seriously, treated me with respect, and placed the demands on me that one places on an equal.

But I'm sure I had a distraught expression on my face, because as we walked, Caro's mom asked me if my parents were very strict. I nodded, my head down. "Don't you worry," she said. "I'll take care of everything. You want to keep coming over to our house, right?"

Her name was Raquel and she told me she worked downtown but didn't like it, and she was taking a class in hair removal so she could set up her own salon.

"I practice on my friends and on myself. Carolina doesn't let me touch her, but if you want, we can try one day . . . Let's see, how are those eyebrows?" she said, smiling, and she came close to peer at my face.

She also told me that she'd lived with Caro for only a short time. She explained it all to me in detail. She had two children, Felipito and Carolita, but she hadn't gotten married, she'd only lived with the kids' dad—that's how she referred to him—for a couple of months, and then she left with them. She'd had money problems and had to leave them at her mother's house for a while, and when their father found out, he had brought them to live with him. Not long ago they'd come to an agreement: he would keep Felipito, and she would keep Carolita.

She was relaxed and cheerful as she spoke, and her lips and laughing eyes gave me the impression that everything she said was half in jest. I liked her, but I also was uncomfortable with her telling me things that I considered private—I wasn't used to an adult talking to me in such a friendly and intimate manner.

They called her La Flaca. She was very tall and thin, which emphasized her thick, black curly hair. She looked very young and she wore a short denim dress, silver earrings in her ears, a gold chain, and several rings. I still liked to play dress-up with my own mother's clothes, though they were mostly long skirts and blouses, shapeless and old, and two-piece work uniforms that were more like medieval armor. My mother said she didn't buy new clothes because she had nowhere to wear them. So as soon as I saw Raquel I fantasized about getting up onto her high heels and looking at myself in the mirror, my chest brimming with her necklaces.

"Oh, you live in the pretty house," she said when we arrived. "Whenever I pass by here I stop and look at it awhile. Did your parents build an addition?"

I looked at her nervously without answering. I was sure that as soon as she rang the bell I would have to once again say goodbye to a friendship.

———

But nothing terrible happened. As soon as my father came out—
frowning, his hands on his hips—Raquel started talking and never
gave him the chance to vent his rage. She introduced herself as his
daughter's friend's mother, and she fell all over herself in apologies.
She said it was all her fault and she could explain everything, in
private. My mother watched from inside, hidden behind the veil
of the curtain, and when the three of us came into the living room
she sent me to my room with a gentle tug on my ear. I didn't know
what Caro's mom told them, but the fact is that they only punished
me with a couple of days without TV. Or my mother did, because
she was the one who disciplined me. My dad was capable of going
weeks without speaking to me, but he never grounded me, he found
it childish.

"You can play with that little girl," said my mother, "but bring her
over here."

I objected, telling her that Caro's house had cable, unlike
ours. That was also unique to my relationship with my mother:
I could complain with her, demand justice and throw tantrums.
Though on that occasion it wasn't necessary to go to such lengths;
she turned out to be unusually understanding, and she eventually
agreed to let me watch cartoons at Caro's house every other day.
I threw myself into her arms and shook my head from side to
side, wheezing like I was blowing out the candles on a birthday
cake. I was going to have a best friend, I told myself. Finally, I
would share my life with another girl like me, and I would have
all those feelings and responsibilities that, I thought, relation-
ships between girls entailed, and that I had so long wished for:

tenderness, secrets, giving oneself unconditionally, grave and
giggly commitment.

✦

Three messages awaited Denise on her computer. Her friend Cris
was insisting again on the party he wanted her to go to with him.

Cris was her only friend. They only saw each other three or
four times a year, but he was her friend. His face was extremely
thin and angular, he'd studied acting, and he constantly reiterated
his hatred for the theater scene. All that afternoon while she'd been
working at the library, he'd been trying to convince her over Facebook chat: enough already with the solitude, they needed to meet
men, preferably cute and with knowledge of Greek and/or Elizabe-
than tragedy. The party would be in Barrio Italia at the studio of
a conceptual artist who had risen to fame after exhibiting a Justin
Bieber fan and her mother in a gallery for three weeks, with a sign
that said they were standing there in exchange for VIP entrance
to the concert. Cris said that on top of the free booze at the party,
they would also be able to network. "It's time to come down from
the bell tower, Sister Wendy," he'd said in his last message. Sister
Wendy was an eighty-two-year-old nun, a hermit and holy virgin
who had prominent front teeth like a rat's. She lived in a mobile
home at the Quidenham monastery of the Barefoot Carmelites,
and she spent six hours of her day contemplating the forest. Lately,
one of Denise's main activities was watching old episodes of Sister
Wendy's 1990s BBC program about art.

"Think of it as a sacrifice. Because this would be a *real* sacrifice—
vows of chastity are getting to be easy for you," wrote Cris.

"Mine is an act of commitment, not obedience or conformity," she replied, quoting Sister Wendy. "Commitment to solitude," she insisted. She opened YouTube, but couldn't think of a song to put on. She felt uncomfortable choosing music, and she preferred to listen to the French girl's groups from the other side of the wall. "You remember the end of *Melancholia*? When they already know that the world is going to end and Kirsten Dunst tells Charlotte Gainsbourg that Earth is evil and that's why they shouldn't regret its disappearance, and that no one will miss it, because there is only life on Earth and we're alone . . . That's how I feel right now."

"How depressing," replied Cris. "Read *The Little Prince*, please.

"Plus," he went on, "only Kirsten Dunst could get away with a phrase like that. With that perfect body, she's got to invent some kind of problem. Plus, she's Mary Jane, and Spider-Man will always rescue her. First let's find ourselves some superheroes, and then we can give in to the pain all you like."

"I don't want a superhero," she wrote, after a few "hahahas." "I don't want to meet anyone, especially not from that world."

Cris replied, "One: That's a lie, you do want to meet someone. Two: The world doesn't matter, what matters is us, it's time for us to be the stars of the show. Three: It doesn't matter if the guy's *cuico*, if you hook up, you can dump him later, break his heart, and it's another victory in the class struggle. Four: I'm sick of writing plays in exchange for congratulations. Networking, now! Five: Do it as a favor to me, no one else will come!!!"

Finally she agreed. Mostly to get free of herself, her nighttime routine. She always had trouble getting to sleep at night. She lay down and stared at the ceiling for several minutes, then changed position and lay facedown with her arms outstretched. With her chest compressed and her heart pounding as if she were jogging, as if she were running away from something that was chasing her, most likely herself. At night she sank down into her thoughts, confronted herself in insomniac monologues. She cornered herself, drowned in her own endless intimacy. Then she'd go out for a bottle of wine and try to calm the anxiety by reading the Old Testament and watching porn.

First, she watched porn. She would open several videos at the same time—nothing out of this world, usually three-ways and orgy parties that were pretty realistic. (She didn't dare see if she'd get excited by Asian women dressed as schoolgirls, the ones who looked very young or who used octopuses as dildos.) She watched the video she liked the most until she managed to come, then closed the computer. Then she picked up the Bible and read a passage from Ezekiel that threatened: "A third part of you shall die of pestilence and be consumed with famine in your midst; a third part shall fall by the sword all around you; and a third part I will scatter to all the winds and will unsheathe the sword after them." Or something along those lines.

It wasn't that she liked watching porn—she thought of it as similar to gulping down a McDonald's combo meal—and nor was she a believer. What she needed was to feel something. She needed pleasure and spirituality, even if it came through a book or a screen. She had to have them close by at night, beside the bed, like scarecrows, but they were ever less effective.

The night before, she had crossed a line. On the way back from the library she'd seen a Muslim family. The sight had struck her as both funny and indignant. They must have been on their way home from the supermarket. The husband was a tall and robust man who walked a few meters ahead, fast and aggressive. The two women, surely his wife and daughter, followed, struggling to keep up with him and carrying some seven bags each. Their heads were covered, their cheeks were flushed with exhaustion, and they wore an expression that Denise dubbed the "virtuous wife." She pitied them, and when she got home she went online to search for information on Islam. From one link to another she arrived at a video of prisoner execution carried out by the Islamic State. She hesitated a second, then she clicked on it.

The conceptual artist's party was an infinitely less torturous panorama than spending the evening watching a man read his own death sentence aloud, utterly calm, and then be decapitated with a hand saw.

She shaved her armpits, and her legs up to her knees. She looked for a dress in the French girl's closet. The one she found most convincing was from Zara, black and long. She looked at herself in the bathroom mirror and confirmed what she already knew. It was too tight, especially at the hips. She was fatter than the French girl, and that was saying something. She didn't feel like trying on any more dresses, so in spite of the night's heat, she put on a green cardigan that would hide the snuggest parts.

When Denise left the apartment, the neighbor from across the landing was still outside. She passed quickly and avoided making eye contact. She saw that the neighbors she called the "stairway couple" were already installed on the landing. Denise raised her eyebrows and wheezed. The stairway couple was a pair of fifty-somethings who carried out their courtship there, between the second and third floors. The woman lived in one of the upstairs apartments with her elderly parents and her son, a nine-year-old boy. As far as Denise understood, the parents wouldn't let the man into the house, and that's why they had to meet up in that absurd way. "Romeo and Juliet of the block," she said to herself, thinking it would be a good joke to share with Cris. Romeo with a potbelly, a plaid shirt with the sleeves rolled up, and dirty jeans; Juliet a stay-at-home mom who lived with her eighty-year-old parents. It made her uncomfortable to go by when they were there, and they seemed to feel the same; their conversation instantly went quiet, and they averted their eyes with a furtive air.

The Islamic family, the condo-fee neighbor, the stairway couple . . . People could be so ridiculous! And the French girl, wanting to meet people, longing for experience! She had no idea, Denise concluded as she reached the gate. She looked for her keys in her bag and realized she'd left without them. She kept searching anyway; dumping out the contents of her bag, she kicked the gate, wheezed again, and sat on the stairs, tired, thinking about how she'd gotten fixed up for a party she didn't want to go to, feeling fat and stupid and also very alone, wanting to laugh and cry at the same time.

After a few minutes she went up to ask the condo-fee neighbor to let her climb over her balcony. She had done it once before, and the neighbor had responded by shaking her head with an expression that said "Just this once."

Resigned, she approached her neighbor, who was out on the landing they shared, her back turned toward Denise. And just then, before she could say a word, Denise saw the moon appear from behind the mountains. The jagged mass of the Andes was just a line that glowed in the darkness, and the moon emerged slowly, yellow and round, near, immense. Denise looked at her neighbor again; she seemed equally caught up in concentration and admiration as she looked out at the scene, leaning on the ledge with a cigarette in hand. And Denise thought—surprised herself by thinking—that maybe this was what her neighbor really did out here every night: wait, alone and in silence, for the moon.

✦

One day Caro and I played a game where we slid down the stairs straddling the railing, and my mother yelled at us. She said that young ladies shouldn't play like that because it was ugly. That same afternoon over supper, my mother asked Caro a lot of questions. Why they lived with her grandparents, where her brother was, how many hours of TV she was allowed to watch, what her dad did for a living, where she got the money for so many albums. All with a curiosity that betrayed a certain disapproval. I was embarrassed, but Caro answered without getting uncomfortable, almost with a hint of impertinence, which was her way of addressing adults.

"He drives a forklift," she replied, referring to her father. I looked at her questioningly, stung that she'd never told me that. "He gives me an allowance, but now that Nicole and I collect the album together, it's easier."

My heart skipped a beat. I lowered my head, waiting for my mother to hit the roof, but she kept talking as if she hadn't heard the revelation Caro had just let slip.

"We don't give Nicole an allowance because we think she's still too little. But her grandparents sneak her money," she said in a reproving voice.

They went on talking about me for a while as if I weren't right there. In my head I was wildly forging and discarding theories. Maybe my mother hadn't heard the bit about the album, or maybe she hadn't understood, maybe she thought Caro shared it with me out of solidarity. Maybe she *had* heard and she was saving the scolding for when we were alone.

"Well," she said when we were finished eating. "Tell your mother to come pick you up tomorrow. I need to discuss a few little things with her."

"A few little things." The diminutive sounded like a death sentence to my ears, and that night I couldn't sleep. I kept thinking about how I could get out of the situation without telling the truth. I decided to ask Raquel for help. I thought of how she seemed to take everything so lightly, and how she'd spoken to me so intimately, and I decided to tell her about the album before she came inside to talk to my mom; I would ask her to help me.

"Easy, easy, it's okay," Raquel told me. "Leave it to me, it'll be our secret."

"You swear?" I demanded, desperate.

"I swear to you."

It was what I needed to hear, and in an impetuous and effusive gesture, I hugged her very tightly. "Thank you," I said. Raquel leaned over a little and hugged me back, and I could feel the lace on her bra against my cheek through her thin blouse.

But I was wrong, once again I was exaggerating. None of the punishments I imagined, which ranged from never watching cartoons again to being forbidden to see Caro, had anything to do with what happened. After several hours of conversation, Raquel came out with my mom and announced that starting then, she was going to watch both Caro and me at our house. That's how they said it, as if we were all part of the same big happy family. After they left, my mom gave me more of an explanation.

"I'm going to pay Caro's mom. Okay? She'll clean and cook in the mornings, and then she'll take care of you two until I get home. It's not a favor, understand? So you have to let me know about anything she does. She knows the rules of the house too, so you behave, and anything she does, you have to tell me. Inappropriate things, like the other nanas have done, remember? Take food home, sleep all afternoon, that kind of thing."

I nodded.

"I chose her because she's your friend's mother and I trust her more, but no matter what, you have to tell me, okay?"

I nodded again. My mother was speaking with that tone of hers, obliging and studiously tender, that she used when she was trying to soften the coldness of her true intentions: orders, warnings, discipline, normalcy. All that maternal tenderness and authoritarianism constructed to hide the fear and vulnerability.

Because of the routine I shared with my parents, it was very easy for me to associate each of them with a certain moment of the day. My father was daytime, the warmth of the morning, the golden sun that made everything visible and mild. My mother was the night, with its blue colors, its cold. And also with its dangers, because my dad got home from work after five in the morning, and my mom, though she didn't complain, walked around restlessly turning the keys in all the locks of the house. She shut herself in and slept fitfully, knowing that at night we were more female than ever, defenseless and alone.

"Now we're going to be like sisters," I told Caro, and although I wanted it so much, I surprised myself by saying it. It scared me to hear.

✦

Denise's friend Cris was extolling the astonishing changes in his social life thanks to Grindr and Instagram.

"Since I'm the gay guy who hates gays, my psychologist and I agreed that I had to integrate more in the community and force myself to meet people."

They were smoking and drinking white wine from plastic cups in the farthest reaches of the inside patio of the house-studio. Cris was wearing some black skinny jeans, sneakers that he classified as "urban," a light blue shirt, a jean jacket, and a necklace of several chains hanging around his neck. Both of them praised the other's outfit, although Cris recommended Denise use more color; color and accessories. "You look like you're in mourning. And as Lady Violet says in the first episode of *Downton Abbey*, 'No one wants to kiss a girl in black.'"

The party had started early at the opening of the artist's exhibition, so it wasn't easy to join in any of the conversations. Nor were they thrilled at the idea, but they had decided they wouldn't give up easily that night. In any case, they were more than happy to spend a little time alone together before starting the hell of socializing, to vent a little by updating each other on the latest events in their tragic existences, analyze and critique the party's clichés, and get just the right amount of drunk.

"How exhausting. I can barely handle Facebook—I get obsessed and it makes me too anxious," said Denise after a long sip of wine.

"It's terrible," Cris agreed. "I swear, I suffer. I suffer with every photo I take of myself and put on Instagram." He made a gesture to suggest true physical pain. "I have to psyche myself up, but now I've figured out how it works. What you have to do is create a story, a story of your life, you know? And in general take pictures of yourself where it's clear you're having fun, hopefully with friends or showing a little skin, so people don't think you're some boring and bitter dude who spends his whole day shut up in the library. Because even though sometimes I complain about everything and spend all day in the library, I'm a really fun person, y'know? Seriously, Denise, I swear, I know that no guy who's gone out with me has gotten bored."

"I never get bored with you."

"Obviously not, we're not boring people. The problem is that no one else knows that, and that's why we have to make it clear. As clear as possible," he stressed, and he lit a new cigarette with the butt of his last. "Of the two of us, you're the one who should have Instagram. I mean, you could at least take photos that are all artistic, in black and white."

"I quit photography. Now I'm a mall librarian."

"I don't understand why you quit, the photos you showed me . . . they were pretty good. That's called self-boycotting. My psychiatrist and I talk about that, too."

"All photographs are good if you have a good camera or a filter," she said coolly, trying to hide the pain she felt at that ill-defined "pretty" that had qualified Cris's "good."

"No, I mean, there was something special about them, something different."

"I hate special, I hate how everyone tries to be different and unique. I want to be as common and everyday as possible."

"Well, let me dispel that little normcore fantasy. What you do with that discourse of yours is just the opposite: You're the weirdest photographer I've ever met."

"It's just, I'm a photographer who hates photography. The only thing I'd like to take pictures of is dead people. Dead or about to die."

"Damn, Denise, so negative."

"How can I be negative? Cameras are all digital now."

"Lame."

"Oh, let me believe in melancholy sadness! Let me believe in destiny!" she said, and raised her glass in a dramatic gesture.

"And let me meet people, otherwise I'll die alone!"

"Well, then I'll come take a picture of you."

They got drunk quickly and looked for an opening in the group standing around the artist. They had to admit that for someone with a name like Demian Blumenthal, he had pretty nice friends. Denise had just convinced herself that she was going to act like it was the best party of her life when Cris told her he was going to the bathroom. He was gone for twenty minutes and returned with an aggrieved face. He explained that he'd been hit with one of his terrible migraines and was leaving as soon as the taxi he'd called arrived. Denise felt a mixture of relief and disappointment.

"Self-boycott?"

"As Tom Branson said: 'I'm sorry, but I can't change into someone else just to please you.'"

She was going to leave with him, but Cris told her not to even think about it. One of them had to come out victorious, and plus, he could tell she was having fun. He took his necklace off and put it over her head.

"I bless you with these, my chains, may you find love this night."

"Will you name me a soldier of love?"

"Judging from that dude you were talking to," murmured Cris, raising his brows and covering his eyes with a hand, "I'd say more like a volunteer."

She decided she was not going to stay alone in a corner, blinking and confused, and she superimposed a radiant expression on her face. She was going to demonstrate that if she stayed here, in this place, it was her own decision, and not a calculation error. She wandered breezily around the party, trying to make her anonymity attractive but teetering too much as she walked. She was possessed of a just slightly excessive euphoria that only caught people's eyes for microseconds. They smiled, yes, but the way you smile at a mime, with fear and a little annoyance. A very young girl hugged her and told her she could see people's auras, and that we all have to keep our hearts open. Denise looked at her in panic and walked quickly away.

In any case, she managed to exchange a few words with three men. The first was the one Cris had mentioned. It was true he wasn't handsome, but he wasn't ugly either, not so ugly, and it wasn't as if she were the prettiest girl at the party; there was a reason he'd dared to talk to her. His head was shaved and he was over thirty. He was a poet but he didn't seem pretentious, and he spoke softly and had a kind of tic that made his eyes unfocus and look toward the ground every once in a while. They laughed together, and at one point, out of nowhere, Denise recited Pavel Sosnovsky's letter in Tarkovsky's film: "I could try not to return to Russia, but that thought kills me . . . because it's not possible that I can never in my life see again the town where I was born, the birch trees, the air of my childhood." The man replied with some verses from "La Jardinera" by Violeta Parra, and things were rolling along nicely until he told her it had been a long time since he'd met someone so special. Denise had to hold back her laughter. "Special," again with the specialness. Leaving aside how clichéd it was, and the fact that they'd only met half an hour before, she didn't want to be "so special." Not for him, not for anyone. She held back her laughter because the poet was clearly insecure, but she fled in less than a minute.

The second man was a journalist with an abundant beard who wore vintage glasses with thick brown frames. She was going to the kitchen to pour more wine when she met him. Just then the song "Boys Don't Cry" came on, and they improvised a dance. When the song was over, he asked her if she wanted to "share universes," and then she did let out a loud peal of laughter, right before she walked away with her glass in hand.

The third guy was a young musician, at least a couple of years younger than her. He was very thin, and wore a suit with vertical stripes that was much too big for him and made him look even thinner. He had long hair pulled back into a ponytail, a mustache, and an earring. She'd watched him for a while earlier as he'd played a gypsy song on the guitar. He wasn't so good-looking, but his attitude made him seem like he was. Finally, she went over to talk to him. The gypsy-musician hardly paid her any attention. They danced for a while, but during all the songs he looked at his dancing reflection in one of the dark windows, his sole intention to seduce himself.

———

At one thirty in the morning, before she left the party, she convinced herself that the place was full of obnoxious people. Hysterics, posers, savages, snobs. And the men . . . As she'd read once: Nothing more pathetic than a man! And there she was, begging for attention! She rummaged through her bag to check, again, what time it was. When she pulled out her cell phone, a slip of paper came with it: a receipt for when she'd had the inner tube changed on her bicycle. It was from a couple of weeks earlier, but she'd kept it because the mechanic wrote "pretty eyes" on the back of it. The first time she'd read it, she had smiled tenderly, thinking how naïve the message was. But now, as she finished her glass of wine before heading home, she thought that was just what she needed. None of that sharing-of-universes stuff, or talk of special people. She wanted someone to tell her something concrete. She wanted someone like that mechanic, someone who worked with his hands and not with words.

Want. She wanted. She needed.

The words resounded in her head as she went out the door to the street. And maybe it was the cool wind that hit her in the face, or the moon that still hung in the sky, full and yellow, or the fact that she was still drunk and was going back to her bed alone at one thirty in the morning, but the words hurt her. She felt again, for the second time that night, humiliated and sick of herself.

She didn't know how to get back to her apartment but she started walking southward, following a route parallel to the mountains. There was a group of three people ahead of her. No one behind her. Nor did she know the name of the street, but it seemed familiar.

The pavement was in poor repair, with patches and holes and deep layers of cobblestones exposed; the cement was new and smooth where she was, and farther on, at the corner, old and cracked. Maybe it wasn't this street, but she'd walked along a similar one, nearby. Some three years earlier, the last time she'd been close to love. She was on her way to an apartment to meet a man, and later that night they found themselves on a roof deck. The man she was with told her a neighbor had given him keys to the roof, saying that no one else had them, but the neighbor trusted him. It was a summer night like this one, with a cold wind on the roof, and she'd thought to herself that she understood the neighbor, because she was probably there for the same reasons. Earlier, they'd drunk champagne and eaten olives, cheese, and salami that the man had bought. Then they went to the edge of the deck and looked to the west, over Vicuña Mackenna. They stood very close together, and Denise felt like her eyelids were trembling. They could hear the traffic from the avenue, and at one point the man said that since he'd never come up here before, he wanted to take a look around. She was left alone, and she looked up at the sky and saw the lights of a plane on the horizon moving in a straight line, neither up nor down. She turned and looked around for the man. She saw him appear from behind the water tank and cross to a small storage room, where he disappeared again. She had a strange feeling; what she'd seen was like a ghost, or like the eddies of sand the wind raised in the Atacama Desert. That man was dust in suspension. She hid behind the water tank and didn't see him again until she went down to the apartment to get her things and leave. He was waiting for her, and before he let her go, he took the shade from the lamp in the living room and put it on her head like a hat, and they both laughed and he kissed her on the mouth. When Denise asked him why he'd done that, the man replied: "It's just that you look like her, you remind me so much of her."

She found a bus stop and sat down. She threw the receipt with the message about her eyes into the garbage. The man on the roof terrace had told her she was strange. He had said it as a compliment, but she didn't like that, either. Special, strange . . . No, she wasn't convinced. Being singular was just that, a single being. The Siberian tiger was special, and it was also alone. She'd been unfair to the poet. He seemed simple, and at the same time he'd understood what she wanted to say about longing, because he'd recited a beautiful poem about the earth. And she had run away from him and she regretted it, but she couldn't go back to look for him now. She didn't do it and she never would. She simply couldn't do it.

The couple was still on the stairs when she arrived. They stopped talking as soon as they saw her. The man was smoking, and he jumped awkwardly to his feet to let her pass. The woman made a gesture as if to hide the glass she held in her hand, and she lowered her eyes. Denise also looked down as she climbed the stairs. When there were only a few more to go before she'd turn and leave the stairway couple behind, the woman's son appeared, the nine-year-old. She had run into the boy before at Don Héctor's shop, buying bread, and also in the hallway, while he played alone with his cars. This time he was holding a Transformer in his hand, and he stood there in front of the couple—Denise behind them—and stared silently, with hatred, at the three of them. Then he ran off and shouted: "Mooooooom! Come inside!"

The idea occurred to her after she closed the door of her apartment and was left in the dark.

Sister Wendy hated her name because of Peter Pan's demure and goody-goody friend. For a time, she'd chosen to be called Sister Michael. Once, people had mocked her after she defined humanity as "beings who pray." What about all those atheists and lazy people in the world who don't pray? "I bet," she replied, "that there has never been a person in the world who, in the middle of the night, hasn't felt that sense of longing, and a feeling of incompleteness and shame. That, to me, is praying."

Denise went quickly down the stairs and proposed the idea to the woman. She looked offended, but after a while, when Denise was already in bed with the computer on her thighs, they knocked on the door.

✦

Raquel was there to meet us the next day. She was wearing the same denim dress she'd had on the first time I saw her. Her hair was pulled back, her eyes lined in brown, and her lips were a soft pink. She brandished the keys with a triumphant smile and opened the gate. She said they'd been waiting for us to eat lunch.

I went up to drop our backpacks in my room. I was struck by how tidy it was, and I looked into my parents' room to see if things were the same there. The curtains and windows were wide open and fresh air was circulating through the room. The bed was made and the floor was free of yoga mats. Everything in place, not a mark on anything.

Neither my father nor I had ever contributed to the household labor. The only thing we did was heat up food at breakfast and lunch. My mother left it prepared in the morning, before she left for work. Milk in the jug, water in the kettle on the stove. Toasted bread with butter on the table, beside the mugs, coffee for him and a healthy Ecco for me. My mother also cleaned the bedrooms and the rest of the house. Sometimes a quick once-over, other times taking the whole afternoon. She'd even polish the little bronze bells that decorated the library, or take the windows out of their frames to clean them on both sides. The cleaning women she hired never lived up to her expectations. Only when I saw those rooms did I realize the danger my friendship with Caro would have been in if my mother didn't like Raquel's style; but with everything so impeccable, that seemed like a ridiculous possibility.

My father was waiting, sitting at the head of the table. I sat at the other end. The kitchen table was rectangular and that was my spot, the only unalterable thing at mealtimes. Caro sat to one side and Raquel, who never stopped talking and laughing as if she were greatly entertained by the situation, served the plates and sat across from her daughter. She'd cooked mashed potatoes and pork chops, my father's favorite, and I wondered whether my mother had suggested it to her.

My father praised the food and Raquel replied: "Thanks, Gonzalo." Then he took out one of the menthol cigarettes he bought at the airport. Raquel teased him, saying they were women's cigarettes, and my father replied very seriously that she should never judge a man for the cigarettes he smokes. For a second I thought his severity was genuine, and I was relieved when I saw him smiling.

That first day Raquel took care of us, things were strange with Caro. Stranger than usual, that is. I knew my friend possessed something disconcerting, something that dazzled me and made me feel like a moth that needed her light, and I also intuited that this was the same quality that made her seem inaccessible. I accepted her coldness, but her indifference often made me feel like a placeholder playmate, a pigeon in a plaza that Caro looked at from time to time, not with a child's curiosity, but with the calm apathy of an adult. I seemed very far from being that special someone for her, the friend who occupied an important part of her heart and thoughts. Whenever we went to her grandparents' house lately she went straight to the stand, divided up the albums—"There's yours"—and sat down on the rug, abstracted, without another word. I obeyed, knelt down beside her, and watched her turn pages monotonously. One day I went over to Raquel's dressing table and applied her lotions to my face. I painted my eyes with blue shadow and my lips an intense red, and I turned around to face Caro, making her mother's bracelets clink together. I wanted Caro to join me, but she barely raised her head to throw me a bored glance.

I dreamed of walking hand in hand with Caro, but she seemed annoyed by physical contact. Any type of contact or communication. We had invented a secret code, but she didn't reply to any of the letters I wrote her so carefully, taking care with my calligraphy and the design of the note and the envelope. Another thing that especially rattled me was the matter of boys. I always had new crushes, and I researched both last names of the boy I liked, his favorite soccer team, and even his parents' names. I wanted to share those secrets with my friend, but it was as if boys didn't exist for her. At least not in the romantic way they existed for me.

Caro distorted the ideal of friendship that I had in my mind, but I'd learned to adapt and to follow the protocol of activities and games she invented. That's why I was surprised at how especially adrift she was that afternoon with Raquel; she followed me around, asking what we should do. I thought she probably didn't like the new situation. Maybe she was annoyed by her mother, who hovered around us constantly and acted as if everything was normal as could be. Raquel suggested we rent a movie, and she didn't mention anything to me about our secret of the albums. While we sat before the TV, she wanted to braid my hair. Caro rolled her eyes and shook her head.

"Let's see what we can do with this short hair . . . I'm going to tell Gonzalo you're too big to have a boy's cut."

"Maybe she likes it that way," Caro said in my defense, angry.

I didn't know what to say. Before, I would have been thrilled, but ever since Caro and I had been friends, my haircut didn't bother me as much.

When we were finally alone, I asked Caro if she was annoyed that her mom was in the house. I made sure not to say "working in the house."

"No," she said, very serious.

"Really?" I asked.

"Really. I'd rather she be here than at her job downtown," she replied with rage, clenching her teeth. I'd never seen her like that. I had the feeling she was confessing something very personal, and I didn't dare ask any more questions.

The days that followed were more normal. We adopted a new

routine. The house smelled like Raquel's Lechuga lotion and Anaïs Anaïs perfume, and it was clean and neat and the lunches were delicious. Caro's mother was the same as always, smiling and pretty. My father was in a good mood and more energetic; the passing hours no longer exhausted him. Caro seemed more concerned about me. She even gave me an album to fill with photos of the places I wanted to visit when we traveled the world together.

We had made the promise to travel after a conversation about a TV program that had left me very confused. My mother had been watching *Special Report* at night, and they had a story on Yugoslav refugees in Chile. It showed their routine in Santiago after they'd escaped war, hunger, and cold. At one point, one of the Yugoslav men yelled at the camera that he wanted to go back; he demanded to be sent back to his country, because in Chile they were all crowded into one room and he didn't have anything, no health care, no education or work. He said the cold was even more unbearable here because they didn't have anything to keep them warm, and life in Chile was disgraceful. I was struck by his voice, raspy like a sick man's, by the rage that brought him to the verge of tears, by his clear desperation when he said he would rather go back to the war than stay in Chile. I asked my mother about the man's words, and she replied that no one chooses where they live.

"But he wasn't born here, they brought him," I insisted.

"He's going to have to get used to it like everyone else," she said.

I couldn't even find Yugoslavia on a map, but that night I had nightmares about it. The next day, I asked Caro what powers she would choose if she were a superhero. She thought about it a few seconds and then replied she'd take anything, that it didn't matter

what your superpower was, as long as you had one. I looked at her
in awe. Had she seen the same program I had the night before? I told
her about the report. I said that I thought we Chileans didn't have
any powers. The Argentines and Brazilians were good at soccer and
had the tango and the samba, I argued. "Yeah," confirmed Caro,
"we had bad luck to be born here. I've always thought so. I used to
think the same thing about being a woman. I thought it would have
been better to be a man, but not anymore."

I agreed enthusiastically. The fact that Caro thought the same
way I did made me feel good, smart and sharp like her. We listed
the advantages—the powers—that other countries had, and to my
joy, we ended by promising that when we grew up we would travel
to see all those countries that were better than ours.

Raquel gave me her old magazines, and between the three of us
we filled the album with pictures of palaces: Buckingham, Monaco,
Zarzuela. Also travel photos of cities and countries. The list of favor-
ites was headed by Athens, Rome, Tokyo, Brazil, Argentina, Russia,
and Yugoslavia. My father asked what we were doing, and when I explained, he looked at me angrily and said we had no idea, that people
lost a lot when they left their countries behind. Raquel calmed him
down, saying he shouldn't get mad, we were only playing. They both
smiled, but when he left, Caro told her mother: "It's not a game."

On the album's last pages I stuck images from a home decor
magazine: a minimalist living room, a futuristic kitchen, a classical
bathroom. I didn't show those to anyone, they were just for me, to
feed my dreams of being an independent adult.

My mom came home and flopped into bed to rest; she didn't even
take her uniform off. Raquel would tell her how the day had gone,
and then she and Caro would leave. Sometimes I went with them, and

other times I stayed to spend time with her. She was very affectionate then, and liked to dance, and sometimes she put on a Los Jaivas cassette and took me by the hands, and we'd spin around the living room. She had more energy in those days, and once she took me shopping downtown. We had tea at the Paula café, as she told me she'd done with her own mother. She bought some moccasins for herself and a parka and some rain boots for me, but told me not to tell my father.

In June there was a teachers' strike. It lasted almost two weeks, and we made the most of that time by going on bike rides in the mornings, my dad, Caro, and me, while Raquel stayed behind to cook lunch. We also went to the playground swings, all four of us. At first my dad treated Caro warily, which always hurt me, but during that unexpected vacation he was warmer; he even got out his checkerboard so they could play. He also told her those strange stories from his religion that he'd read to me, like the one about the man who tried to hide from God. One afternoon he came down with his camera and used a whole roll of film taking pictures of us. More albums to fill. Caro asked to see it. It was a very simple Olympus, but my dad taught her to focus. Finally he put the camera on the curved edge of the TV and set the timer. He ran to sit next to the three of us on the living room sofa. "To immortalize the moment," he said. I took the chance to hold Caro's hand, and she closed her fingers around mine.

✦

Denise opened the door in pajamas, or rather in the long, stained old shirt that she used as pajamas. She didn't even turn on the living room light: she knew it was them.

The knock on the wood, slow and hesitant. The fact that they didn't ring the doorbell—it couldn't be anyone else. She could see them, the silhouette of a couple backlit against the landing's light, but realized they probably couldn't see her. She apologized with an awkward laugh and turned on the light, and then she felt even more awkward and nervous, because she realized she was in her nightshirt, her "pajama by default," which left her almost naked in front of them, suggestive. Because of course, that's how they would think of her: the young and promiscuous neighbor—though they had never seen her come home accompanied by a man, or anyone. A girl newly perverted, who received them in pajamas.

"Come in," Denise said, trying to appear composed in spite of her bare feet and thighs. And she laughed again, but this time in a defiant way, as if saying: *Come in, come in, I have nothing to be ashamed of, nothing to make me blush.*

The couple entered, or rather, took a few steps forward. The three of them looked at each other in silence, standing there face to face. Studying each other, Denise thought; at least, she was certainly studying them. It was clear they still hadn't made a decision—none of them had, she thought. Most likely, after discussing it for a while, the stairway couple had come to the conclusion that they would test the waters, yes, they would stop by and see how it was, and once they were in the apartment, they would come to a conclusion. It would be easy; the setup of the place, their neighbor's attitude, her tone of voice, the looks they would exchange, and the good or bad feeling they got would tell them whether to accept the proposal. For her part, she could also back out, pretend she hadn't meant *that*, make the excuse that she was drunk.

They didn't know each other; they looked each other up and

down, and Denise's scale started to tip. No, it hadn't been a good idea. Her opinion of them, the idea she'd formed on seeing them in the stairway was, well, that they were vulgar, but she'd invited them to her apartment anyway, and now it was blowing up in her face.

It's one thing to relate a grandfather with death, quite another to smell the old man's stench and listen to him rave.

"Juan Carlos." The man introduced himself, holding out his hand. A small but thick hand, rough to the touch, with the lines on the palm black as if tattooed. His nails were also black, a tidy black that made Denise conclude that he must work with his hands, and with grease and oil and machines. Maybe he was a mechanic, maybe he wasn't very meticulous with soap, or maybe no soap existed that could really get his hands clean.

"Denise," she replied doubtfully, as if she weren't sure of her name.

"Denise?" asked Juan Carlos, with a sly air. "You sure? What, don't you like your name?"

The woman stayed back, didn't introduce herself. She kept silent, mysterious, as if she didn't want to be part of this negotiation, or as if she were merchandise to be traded and couldn't voice an opinion on the matter. Maybe she just thought that after they'd been neighbors so many years, Denise knew her name, just as she knew about her misfortunes and romantic affairs.

But not Juan Carlos, no; he was a man of introductions, a man with nothing to hide, a man you couldn't get anything past. The opaque skin of his face was pocked with acne scars. He had a beard

of a day and a half, the kind that looks like stains or dirt. So his face
was in harmony with his hands: hardened, unpolished wood. Denise also noticed his hair more than she had before, black and generous, and his thick, broken nose that crossed his face in diagonal, and
the wrinkles around his eyes, also very black, as if soot or machine
grease—she was sure he worked with grease—had built up there.
He looked at her with a hard expression, and she thought it was
probably always like that, stony, the face of a boy whose father beats
him, but who understands and still loves the man, is even grateful
for the punishment. He had surely been brought up in the country.
A *huaso*, a hick, that's who she had invited into her house, a hick
who hated Santiago and its inhabitants, with all their cement stairs.

"You've traveled a lot, looks like," he said to Denise with a
mocking tone, and he cocked his head toward the big world map
stuck to the wall, marked with colored pins. The pins held up photos of countries visited, and like the rest of the decoration in the
living room, it was the French girl's work.

"Yes," she replied.

"And? Has it been useful?" he asked contemptuously. Obviously, because he was a man who weighed things according to their
usefulness. A vertical man, immovable, from a single land, a man to
whom travel must have seemed almost like an insult.

"Of course," replied Denise, and she added a tender smile just
to irritate him.

"How nice," he rushed to say, to put an end to the conversation.
He went on examining the apartment suspiciously, while he rested
his hand, more protective than affectionate, on the woman's thigh.

The neighbor lady was wearing a very short jean skirt and a
black jacket, both of them too tight. Her hair was long and brown

and pulled back into a ponytail, and she hid her eyes behind some thick-rimmed glasses. If Denise had her doubts about Juan Carlos, the neighbor lady really repelled her. She was the kind of woman Denise hated and criticized, a woman who needed a man for introductions. Diminished to the point that she hunched over, though she was tall. An expression that was permanently anxious and grateful. Pale, a woman who in spite of her dark, reddish skin always looked pallid, milky.

"Well now, what's the deal here?" asked Juan Carlos, and Denise found herself forced to decide, and as she explained it to him she decided on a yes, even if it was only so as not to let herself be cowed, not to seem indecisive, to be equal to the man's assertiveness and confidence. Juan Carlos asked a couple of questions, and she replied to them. It was like a competition, which of the two had the straightest spine, and somehow the rivalry linked them together, as if they were father and daughter or big brother and little sister.

Ignoring the woman, they walked to Denise's room.

What Juan Carlos couldn't hide was his surprise at the mess and the lack of decoration in the room; compared with the living room, it was a wasteland. Denise smiled faintly and shrugged. She picked up her computer and blurted, "Well, I'll leave you two alone," which didn't make sense, since Juan Carlos was the only one there. Then she shut herself away in the French girl's room.

They lay on Denise's single bed, and Denise lay in the French girl's double bed. She didn't close the door, and neither did the neighbor lady. Denise was sure it had been the woman's decision to leave it

half open, because she was the last one in, and because it was co-
herent with her personality, the one Denise imagined she had. A
woman who didn't close doors, so no one would think badly of her,
even when it was clear what she was doing. A woman who didn't
face facts, who spoke softly, a Goody Two-shoes.

She listened to them that first night; all she could do was listen.
She had heard the French girl have sex before. Although hers were
fairly pleasant little cries, soft and rhythmic, tinkling, they always
made Denise very nervous, almost to the point of desperation. She
hid under the sheets with the computer on and the volume turned
all the way up in her headphones, and she concentrated on Sister
Wendy's South African accent or on the moans of some Belorus-
sian porn actress.

The sounds of Juan Carlos and the neighbor were different. The
first noise she heard was metal against wood, and it almost seemed
like she could already see them: before anything started, Juan Carlos took off his watch and placed it heavily on the nightstand. Then
there were some muffled sounds of recognition, and then a ripping.
She didn't hear shouts or blows, but the sound of their heaving bodies, their moans and panting, certainly came from pain, from an
untamable affliction without concessions or symmetry. As if the
sex, the love, were something that had to be endured, as if the suffering were a discipline and a gift. Denise let herself be carried
along by that sound, and she breathed deeply and fell asleep almost
without realizing it.

The next morning she found the room empty and the bed made. Very well made, smooth but not too tight. Docile, like the neighbor lady, because it was clearly her work. The blanket stretched meticulously, but also sensitively—Denise would never be able to make a bed that way. She carefully brought her face close to the bed to catch any trace of their scent.

In her first two years in the building, every night between twelve thirty and one in the morning she'd heard a consistent noise, a rhythmic tapping that came every four counts on the ceiling of her room. Denise didn't know if the layout of the apartments was the same on every floor, or who lived in the one just above her bedroom, but she imagined, from the sound, that it was someone sitting and bouncing a tennis ball. She knew it was a pretty silly idea—who would sit there in the middle of the night and do that for thirty minutes? At first the sound annoyed her and she wanted to go complain, but over time, when she found an explanation—invented an explanation—it stopped bothering her. She imagined a man, she liked to imagine a man with a neutral expression on his face, neither happy nor sad, but concentrated, methodical, like the sound and the pauses of the ball as it bounced.

Juan Carlos and the neighbor lady visited her every three days. They knocked on the door at eleven thirty at night and they left at one in the morning, just as they had agreed.

She opened the door to them in a gray sweatshirt over her pajamas. Juan Carlos shook her hand. "Hello, Denise," he'd say, emphasizing her name with an insidious tone, as if he wanted to let her know that he knew a terrible secret about her. "Hello, Juan Carlos," she replied with forced naturalness. The upstairs neighbor greeted her with a nod of the head, always behind Juan Carlos and carrying a bag in her hands: clean sheets. Denise thought that the first time, after the Friday when she'd heard them, her neighbor would look nervous and ashamed. But it was just the opposite. Beneath her usual reserved attitude was a certain affirmative energy. Not exactly pride, but stubbornness. Over time Denise began to think of her as a pilgrim, a walker who followed her man down the road, but who isn't any less valuable or brave than him—quite the contrary. Behind her glasses and her cornered posture, her naïveté and her tight clothes, there lived an intrepid woman.

Juan Carlos would offer an opinion about the weather or the news, but he never asked Denise how she was or what she thought. He wasn't interested in knowing about her life, and he didn't try to make friends. Why would he? Denise didn't like Juan Carlos, but she respected him for that. It was a relief that not everyone wanted to go around smiling and opening their hearts.

The formalities of their greeting in the living room lasted under five minutes. Then Denise headed to the French girl's room and they went to Denise's. One room next to the other, with the doors half open. Every three days.

Once in the room they always acted in the same way, following an unvarying order, as if it were a play. The prelude was a conversation, which Denise was left out of because they spoke very softly, almost in whispers. It must have been a trivial chat in which they shared their small emotions of the day, their ordinary routines, but maybe, between the high price of a kilo of avocados and the unbearable February heat, a confession glinted, some family drama of the upstairs neighbor's, or a lustful proposition that guided them to the next act. The fact was, Denise still didn't know anything about them. She didn't know what they did for a living, what kind of music they liked, what news channel they preferred. Did they have problems with ex-spouses, or were they fifty-something singles? Why weren't they allowed into the woman's house? Why didn't they go to his? She found it funny that they were so inhibited with her when it came to a simple conversation, and so unrestrained when it came to the noise they made later. Although for Denise, the whole thing made sense because of that. She thought it showed a certain mutual trust, trust between her and the couple. Trust was only possible when you didn't know everything about the other person.

Denise got up from the French girl's bed after hearing the watch hit the nightstand, two things as naturally connected as a nail in a board. Why did he do it? Was it just for comfort, or was there more to it? She had seen many professors do the same thing at the institute. Before starting classes they took off their wristwatches and placed them on the table. In their case it was so they would know when class was over, but she wasn't sure of Juan Carlos's reasons. Did he set the watch down so he could keep an eye on the time, or so he could forget about it?

She watched them with the help of a hand mirror, crouched down and hidden outside her bedroom door. They kept a tenuous light switched on and it shone onto Denise's face through the fifteen centimeters that the neighbor left to her. Nor was the sex very informative. As she spied on them, Denise was still aware of a certain restraint in the couple. In their positions, the way they touched each other. They kept a certain distance between them, provocative in its reserve. They went down a winding path as they took their clothes off, an incomplete expedition, and neither of them was ever completely revealed to the other. Much was hidden from Denise, too, because of her restricted view. She couldn't access the kind of close-ups she was used to from porn. The neighbors' performance was always elusive. But she liked it. She'd always thought of herself as an amateur street photographer, and she liked to feel as if she was in a photography studio, one where the photographer couldn't give orders, couldn't demand "Show me!" She found it entrancing that not everything came into view, that it wasn't a shop window and something stayed inaccessible and hidden. It made it more exciting.

After all, their old bodies weren't exactly a delight in themselves. Juan Carlos was fat, although his skin was still taut, cultivated by the years of physical labor she was still sure his job entailed. His chest and belly had something simian about them, his arms were curved and hairy, his chest smooth. The neighbor lady's body was much more flaccid, fallen. She had a cesarean scar that divided her belly—another boundary—and enormous breasts that Juan Carlos could hardly cup in his small hands. Denise thought he would be the one on top or behind the whole time, dominating her, but she was the one who mounted him, directing him in his caresses and touching herself. Still, he didn't seem subordinate. Juan Carlos maintained that awkward vigor, that determination he had when he shook Denise's hand in greeting, when he moved straight-backed through a house that wasn't his, taking it over with every step. He had the same determination when he spoke, seeming to say—from deep within him and not without arrogance——that there was only one right way to do things.

They were quite conventional, didn't move excessively or try different or difficult poses. They didn't adorn the sex. They were monotonous and they took their time touching each other; they went slowly, following their own rhythm. But that didn't mean they lacked expression or enthusiasm——it was clear they desired each other and felt enormous pleasure. And Denise also liked that; it seemed even more romantic that they were systematic. They didn't need to try their luck with new positions, because they knew what satisfied them. They were predictable as a ceremony, and she could anticipate what was coming and attain a certain exalted state, like in a ritual.

The couple performed and Denise read their actions. And as she concentrated on them, interpreting them, she managed to let go, she stopped thinking about herself and finally got free of herself. She didn't feel alone or distant. She was not an invisible watcher, because every once in a while the neighbor lady looked at her. And although to Denise she appeared bewildered and tired, her gaze was not a transparent look toward an indeterminate place; she looked directly at Denise. It was an intelligent and complicit look, dark and painful, and Denise returned it. She observed them with her obscene, compassionate eyes, completely entranced, relieved, feeling that she was here with them, that she was part of their intimacy, that she belonged to them, that she was there, really there.

✦

One day at the beginning of September, the religion teacher didn't show up and they let us go home early. I went to Caro's class to ask if I should stay until she got out, but she told me to wait for her at my house.

The gate was unlocked, so I went in. I knocked on the door but there was no response. I went back to ring the bell, but before hoisting myself up—the lighted doorbell my father was so proud of was installed high up on the gate, hidden behind the climbing vines so it wouldn't get stolen—it occurred to me that I'd better not wake my father if he was still sleeping. I crossed the patio to the kitchen and climbed in through one of the windows. The house was in silence and the sink was full of the dirty breakfast dishes. I went toward my room, heading up the stairs, and on the first steps I heard laughter, and my father's voice, and Raquel's, too.

For some reason, I stopped. I tried to hear what they were saying, but I couldn't make it out. I kept going up, but for some reason I did it carefully, maintaining the silence of the house. I kept going to my parents' room in the same way, without taking off my backpack, on tiptoe, holding my breath. For some reason. Later I would wonder why I acted like that. My father distrusted people and believed in energy and vibrations. I'm not sure my attitude was an inheritance of that idea, but I guess something in the silence and the tone they were speaking in alarmed me and made me act like an intruder.

The door was half open and I pushed it a bit, gently, and that little space was enough to let me see the reflection of my father and Raquel in the mirror by the door. A mirror that, like other objects in the house, was a kind of icon, a symbol of the room, of my parents' marriage and my home, the one they built by filling it with things. It was rectangular, full-length, and I used to look at myself in it when I played dress-up in my mother's clothes. And there they were, Raquel and my father, lying in the bed half naked. Just resting, killing time, lazing as if it were a Sunday morning. Their pose didn't denote the nervous urgency of something secret; they weren't even embracing, they didn't feel the need to cling to each other or to a moment that could be the last. They laughed, and kissed from time to time. My dad had a bit of stubble and Raquel's makeup was faded. I watched them; I didn't run away. I stayed there for a couple of minutes as though hypnotized, as though blinded, as if all my father's light, all the light he was and that made things visible, that illuminated my own image, were dazzling me. Blinded, dazed by the light, a couple of minutes, several minutes. Invisible.

I closed the door and left with the same stealth as before. Not because I was in some kind of shock; I simply didn't want to bother my father. Habit, the rule against interrupting him during the morning, won out over my surprise.

I went back to school and asked Caro if we could visit her grandma.

My father had told me once that there were two kinds of houses: those that were owned and those that were rented. "You can tell right away," he said, pointing to one where the paint was peeling on the wall and the fence. "It's not worth keeping it up if it's not yours." He added that people who lived in rented houses didn't take care of the front yard, or have a good hose, a doorbell that shone in the dark, or any of the things we had. "You can tell, you can tell," said my father. For him, Caro's grandma's house would fit with the "rented" type. The cement floor had holes, and the countless flowerpots were filled only with dry earth, seemingly proving him right. But the truth is that her corner house didn't entirely fit either of his categories, because the patios of rented houses were always empty, and Caro's grandma's was overflowing with objects: a rusted water heater, a calendar with a woman in a bathing suit, a white stove, gas cylinders, wooden tables and chairs handmade especially for the patio or inherited from the interior. And it's not that I was surprised by that. My only reason for mentioning it is that I am sure none of those things are there now, and that everything is different. And I can only call up the memory of that patio as it was that day, when I stayed beside Caro's grandmother and the dogs, safe, for the whole afternoon, as we let the shade of the arbor cover us while we clung to her.

The next day I didn't visit Caro at school. It wasn't my intention to avoid her, it was just that I'd had nightmares about *The Knights of the Zodiac*, and I spent all of recess sleeping on a bench. Nor did I plan not to talk to her while we walked home through the alleyways, or to refuse to eat the steak *a lo pobre* that Raquel made that afternoon. I felt a lethargic weariness, the kind that arises from the freedom of doing nothing.

I went on like that for three days. Exhausted, but with a sharp pain in my jaw and the desire to cry every time my eyes met my father's, or when I saw Raquel go by carrying the hot water for his shave. I was disgusted by all that intimacy of theirs, full of jokes and compliments on the food. That brash and shameless happiness they shared, the joy that floated around them like the morning torpor in my father's room, and that left me out—me and my mother. Their closeness made me sick, the pleasure they must have shared.

The only time I ever saw my parents kiss with tongues was on vacation, two years before. I remembered perfectly because that was also the day I found out how babies were really made. A beach friend who wore braces told me. We were sitting in the sand and the saliva in her braces glinted in the sun. She whispered in my ear how the man stuck his penis in the woman's vagina, and I felt her hot hand on my ear and I turned immediately to look at my parents, who were a few yards away under a sun umbrella. My dad was trying to kiss my mother from an awkward position, and she was resisting. They realized I was looking at them and they started to laugh nervously. I didn't feel disgust, but their attitude seemed strange. They looked very clumsy, laughing with their lips stretched and their tongues half out.

I hated Raquel now, but I tried not to look at her with rage; I couldn't stop being the obedient girl who respected adults. Above all, I hated her because she had kept my secret about the album and I owed her one, and our secrets joined us together. Although there was also the possibility that she'd betrayed me: maybe some morning, lying there so comfortably, she'd told my father about the fuss I'd made over that childish nonsense.

I hated her because she lied to my mother just like I did.

One afternoon that we spent in her room, Caro invited me to watch TV. As always, she pressed 11 on the remote control, but I grabbed it from her hands and changed the channel. *Buffy the Vampire Slayer* was on. I told her cartoons were for little kids, and I looked at her as if she were a traitor.

On his free Tuesday, my dad suggested we go out. From the doorway of my bedroom, he insisted: "Just the two of us." I shook my head. "Come here," he ordered, and he rested his hand on my shoulder.

"What's going on, Nicole?" he asked, trying to be understanding.

"Nothing," I said, averting my eyes.

"Why are you so angry lately? Tell me. You can tell me anything."

I still wouldn't look at him, and I didn't answer. He was also quiet.

"Are you jealous of Carolina? Are you jealous because lately the three of us do a lot together?"

I shook my head, looking at him with eyes full of rage.

"You have to learn to share, Nicole," he went on in his tone of forced comprehension. He knelt down while he ran his hand up and down my back. "She doesn't have a dad like you do."

"Yes she does! He drives a forklift!"

"Yes, sure she has one, but not like you do, understand?"

I nodded.

"I'm not jealous," I said, and maybe I sounded convincing, because he smiled at me.

I looked him in the eyes, and I remembered the time I'd seen him cry, the only time. We'd gone several weeks without speaking. I don't remember why, but the fact is we fought and he stopped speaking to me, as he did when he wanted to punish me. That time, though, I imitated his technique: I also acted offended and refused to talk to him. I stayed strong for the first time, and I lasted several days. One afternoon my father came into my room and knelt down in front of me. He took my hands and asked me to forgive him. Then he hugged me and started crying. I stayed stiff, not sure what to do. He cried like a child and he didn't stop begging me to forgive him and to please start talking to him again. I felt very sad remembering that moment, but it also calmed me.

I flung my arms around his neck and started to shake. I felt like I was fainting.

"Do you feel bad, Nicole?" he asked.

I lunged at him and kissed him on the mouth.

He took me by the shoulders and pushed me away, surprised; we didn't usually demonstrate our affection physically.

"Is that it? Are you sick?"

I felt a burning in my throat and waves of cold ran over my whole body. Right when my father said those words I started to get sick, and I felt soothed, because until that point in my life illness had always been a safe place: dreamy days when I didn't go to school and I received attention and affection in the form of soda crackers with jam and orange juice. Yes, that's what I had to do, give in, surrender to the sickness.

My father moved a little farther away. He checked for hot sweat under my armpits and felt my forehead, and I smelled the tobacco and mint of his fingers.

"You seem to have a little fever. I'm going to tell Raquel."

I left the room and ran straight into Caro. My friend. I hadn't thought about her much in all this time. It's not that I felt aversion toward her like I did Raquel, I was just concerned with other things. Caro came over uncertainly and proposed we play on the stair railing. I accepted, but all it took was to see her sliding down with her legs open to make me refuse to keep playing. Caro asked me why, and I gave her a hard look and said:

"Because it's disgusting and girls shouldn't do it."

"What do you want to play?" she asked, pleading for my company.

"Barbies."

We went up to my room and sat on the carpet, shielded behind the bed. I made a house for Barbie out of books and boxes. I folded a towel in four parts to make a double bed. I gave Caro instructions in an angry, bored voice, as if any contribution from her infuriated me, letting her know I was in charge of the game. I picked up my Barbie and a souvenir someone had given me some years earlier: a soda can disguised with a charro hat, dented in the middle, with plastic googly eyes and a mustache over the opening for a mouth. The Mexican can would be the man, because I didn't have a Ken. Caro watched from a certain distance, cowed by my attitude. I took Barbie's clothes off and laid her on the towel-bed, put the can on top of her, and started to rub them together and imitate the sounds I thought couples made. It was a game I sometimes played, but I had never shown her.

"You be the man," I ordered her.

"I don't want to play. That really is disgusting."

I smiled mockingly. "That's what you think, because you don't know anything."

"Why are you treating me like this? What have I done to you?"

I looked at her for a moment. I still had the Barbie and the can in my hands.

"Nothing, you haven't done anything, you're just boring. Playing with you is boring," I answered, and I realized it was true, that for a while now she had bored me. But I also realized something else. Caro was looking at me with weepy eyes, and that comforted me. In the depths of my heart, it comforted me. I had so wished for and sought out her attention and recognition, and I no longer needed it. I didn't need Carolina, and for some reason I felt better hurting her.

"I bore you? Now I bore you?" asked Carolina in a trembling voice. "It's because now I'm the maid's daughter, right? That's why?"

I saw my friend's hurt expression, and I twisted my mouth into a cruel smile.

No, Caro didn't deserve it. Neither of us deserved it.

"Yes, that's why," I told her, relentless. "Because you're the maid's daughter, and because you're poor and you don't have a dad."

Carolina ran out of the room and I sat there with the Barbie in my hand, feeling triumphant and at the same time terribly humiliated. I looked for the album of travel pictures among my things. I tore the pages up and scattered the pieces over the floor. I don't remember much more; after that, I got sick.

My convalescence wasn't what I'd expected. More nightmares. I saw Pompeii burning and people screaming and turning into statues, and those dreams got mixed up with the idea of being sick. Delirious with fever, I thought what I had was meningitis. I thought I was going to die, and I cursed Caro between dreams for having infected me. The few minutes I was conscious, I saw Raquel. She gave me pills, took my temperature, or caressed my head, and all I could think was that I had meningitis and I was going to die, and that it was Caro's fault.

When I woke up the house was silent. I got out of bed and looked out the window. The clock radio said 12:45. I felt lost, as if I were emerging from a long coma, but I walked calmly, rested, to my parents' room. The door was closed, and I pressed my ear to it and heard a strange sound on the other side. I looked fearfully at the door, but I told myself that this time I would be brave and I'd go in. I would face whatever I found in there. I threw it wide open and I found Caro. She was sitting in front of the mirror with a tube of lipstick in her hand, one that could have been Raquel's or my mother's, and her whole face was painted red. And when I saw her reflection, her skin red like raw meat as if she were burning, I screamed. I screamed in terror, and Caro also started screaming. We both screamed, looking at each other in the mirror, we screamed and cried for help as loud as we could.

✦

She'd gone back to her nighttime walks. Again, she wandered through Ñuñoa's streets. Dark streets, because the leafy branches of the trees attenuated the streetlights. Silent, because the walls of the houses and old apartments were thick, and didn't let the sound of the TV, the music, or the fights filter out. The old people were asleep at that hour, and the models were making tea in their houses.

She walked decisively, as if she had somewhere to be or a destination in mind, as if she were walking a dog, though she doesn't have a dog or need one. Her steps roamed with determination. Eating an apple granola bar, she passed a construction site and stopped to look through a hole in the black mesh around the perimeter. She saw a deep, enormous pit with wooden boards and iron mesh sticking out. On one side there was a long table with a black plastic sheet over it. It surely covered the workers' tools or their cups and plates, but it also accentuated a hexagonal shape and made the table look like a coffin. That's what she saw: a coffin beside a pit. There were also large rocks and a lot of dirt. She wondered what they did with all that earth, and she noticed the tracks left by the wheel of a back-hoe: deep, horizontal waves. She thought of a dinosaur footprint, the damp step of a *Tyrannosaurus rex*. A good setup for a photograph, she told herself. During the day, with the laborers at work, it would also be a good scene. Maybe a bit clichéd, but it would surely be a good photograph. A couple of big old houses had been torn down to dig a deep hole, and soon the hole would also disappear, replaced by a building of twenty-four floors, and that wouldn't be eternal, either. Yes, she should take a picture, and it would be a good picture. She stood there looking for several minutes and thinking about a few ideas for framing and spacing. She had to accept that when she was little, she had in fact dreamed of working for *National Geographic*, of traveling the world taking well-focused pictures with just the right light.

She sat on a bench. She wanted to look at the people passing by, but no one passed.

Sometimes that was enough. To sit on a bench and look around while the streets emptied and everything got quiet and dark. She had spent hours not doing anything but waiting for night to fall, for the background to change. With the granola bar in her hand, static, idiotic, like someone who goes to the theater just to see the changes in lighting. No action, just the passage from light to darkness.

There were times when it was enough, but it was also true in part that she did it because she didn't want to go back to her bed and lie down and look at the white ceiling of her room, smooth and impassive, empty, one big no.

She thought of the couple again.

She thinks: Well, in any case the French girl will be back soon from her trip.

She remembers her last conversation with the upstairs neighbor.

"I don't know what to say." That's what she said after the neighbor thanked her. It was the only thing that occurred to her in the moment, and maybe it was the right reply: not saying anything. Not because she didn't care—the truth was, she couldn't stop thinking about them. But it seemed so obvious that it was unnecessary, that it would only be out of politeness.

They didn't owe her anything.

She'd wanted to say something to her neighbor. Her eyelids had trembled and she'd wanted to say: "If you like, one day you two could come for dinner. Or it could be just you and me, if you want." She didn't dare. It didn't make sense, and anyway, she was sure the neighbor lady would refuse. But she still practiced in her mind the best way to suggest it, one that would sound informal and inspire trust: "We could have dinner one of these days"; "How about we get together for tea some afternoon, the three of us?"

She didn't say anything and she stood there, hunched over just like the upstairs neighbor, waiting for her to say goodbye. Waiting for the final moment.

"Do you always wear that gray sweatshirt?" asked the woman. "I dress like this because I think it's what Juan Carlos likes," she added with a self-conscious smile.

Denise swallowed and turned her face away. Her eyes were damp and she opened her mouth and tried to contain herself. She saw the reflection of the two of them in the windowpane, the whole room projected and floating on the other side, and the neighbor lady came closer, hugged her. Denise stood with her hands hanging down. She couldn't turn her face, but she closed her eyes.

"It's not because of you," said the neighbor. "I have to find another place, but it's not because of you . . . That's just how it is."

Denise nodded.

Juan Carlos shouted from the hallway: "Ready?"

She goes back to walking, she passes behind the House of Culture. A statue of a naked man is lying on the ground, split in half. It's white, Renaissance-style. Until recently, it was whole. Really, she doesn't know how recently, because she doesn't remember the last time she saw it. Its spotlight is on, but now shines only on the legs. A fallen man; she stops to see it better. Frightening.

She thinks: I don't know them, they don't know me. That's the only thing I know. I don't know them, but I did manage to understand some things.

"Carolina?" yells Juan Carlos. "Are we going or not?"

Carolina. Finally, her name. The upstairs neighbor finally had a name.

Denise asks herself: Do I miss them?

She replies: I lost them.

Before she left, the neighbor lady's eyes shone behind her glasses. Why? What was that shine? Hope, or poor judgment? Both?

How do I walk? she wonders. With hope or good judgment?

"Lucky me," Sister Wendy used to say. Lucky that God allowed her to live in isolation and drink as many cups of coffee as were necessary to stay alert to him, her Creator. Lucky that she wasn't obligated to be a friend, a wife, a mother. *I'm afraid that people haven't meant much to me in life.*

She wasn't so sure she could say the same. She had always been a solitary person, yes, but the tension in her heart was still there. A few months back, her mother had started selling Herbalife. Every time she called, she tried to convince Denise that those shakes would change her life. "Start by drinking more water. At least drink water!" she begged. Two liters of water were her solution for the world's problems. And maybe she was right, maybe someone should tell that to the armed Islamic State.

She had never fallen in love, she was alone, she felt isolated, trapped, she didn't belong anywhere, she hadn't achieved much . . . there were worse things, people who suffered for real, people who lost their houses in a fire or a flood. But that was no consolation, not a clean one at least, one free of any selfishness. It wasn't that she felt like she would go crazy, at least not before midnight, but she had to admit that the current state of her life did not strike her as good. Still, she didn't give in to sadness as she walked. She was full of free will. She had made decisions, she owned her failures, and no one could say that failure didn't take effort or sacrifice. Her defeat belonged to her, like her isolation and abstention. And the recognition of that was a kind of win, was it not? Would her mother accept recognition as a win? Would she accept it herself?

She had once dreamed of being a photographer for *National Geographic*, and now she had to find some way to go back to her apartment and manage to sleep.

Lucky me, she told herself.

On her way home, she again met the Muslim family walking down the sidewalk. Just like the last time, the man went ahead and the two women behind, carrying supermarket bags. Denise looked at them, and recognized that the first time, she hadn't really looked. The mother, the one who must have been the mother, was young, much younger than the husband. She must have been Denise's age.

Denise liked the scarf covering her head, a pale pink with white vines printed on it. She was going and they were coming. And when they passed each other, Denise smiled at the mother. Not a cynical smile; she didn't pity her. And the mother smiled back. A subtle smile, but full of conviction.

She turns the computer on and flops on the bed. A dog barks, and another responds. She listens to a car brake abruptly, hears the tires squeal. She hears women laughing and a little girl screaming. The sound of a kettle boiling, like a train reaching a station. The murmur of many televisions and lightbulbs and computers turned on. She is still lying on her bed with her eyes fixed on the ceiling, static. The sounds take their time, they approach and move away. She hears her own breathing over all that noise, which in a way composes a kind of silence. She is unable to close her eyes. The ceiling is a neutral white. She hears a knock at the door. Three quick raps, so fast they are transparent. She sits up straight. Turns her ear toward the door. Waits. Listens. Maybe it's just one more noise in the routine sounds of this building, of any regular building like hers. She listens. Maybe it's her imagination, or a joke, a man bouncing a tennis ball. She listens. Maybe someone is knocking on the door of another apartment. After all, she can't be the only one waiting for someone. Can she?

Oneworld, Many Voices

Bringing you exceptional writing
from around the world

The Unit by Ninni Holmqvist (Swedish)
Translated by Marlaine Delargy

Twice Born by Margaret Mazzantini (Italian)
Translated by Ann Gagliardi

Things We Left Unsaid by Zoya Pirzad (Persian)
Translated by Franklin Lewis

The Space Between Us by Zoya Pirzad (Persian)
Translated by Amy Motlagh

The Hen Who Dreamed She Could Fly by Sun-mi Hwang
(Korean) Translated by Chi-Young Kim

Morning Sea by Margaret Mazzantini (Italian)
Translated by Ann Gagliardi

A Perfect Crime by A Yi (Chinese)
Translated by Anna Holmwood

The Meursault Investigation by Kamel Daoud (French)
Translated by John Cullen

Laurus by Eugene Vodolazkin (Russian)
Translated by Lisa C. Hayden

Masha Regina by Vadim Levental (Russian)
Translated by Lisa C. Hayden

French Concession by Xiao Bai (Chinese)
Translated by Chenxin Jiang

The Sky Over Lima by Juan Gómez Bárcena (Spanish)
Translated by Andrea Rosenberg

The Baghdad Clock by Shahad Al Rawi (Arabic)
Translated by Luke Leafgren

The Aviator by Eugene Vodolazkin (Russian)
Translated by Lisa C. Hayden

Lala by Jacek Dehnel (Polish)
Translated by Antonia Lloyd-Jones

Bogotá 39: New Voices from Latin America
(Spanish and Portuguese) Short story anthology

Last Instructions by Nir Hezroni (Hebrew)
Translated by Steven Cohen

Solovyov and Larionov by Eugene Vodolazkin (Russian)
Translated by Lisa C. Hayden

In/Half by Jasmin B. Frelih (Slovenian)
Translated by Jason Blake

What Hell Is Not by Alessandro D'Avenia (Italian)
Translated by Jeremy Parzen

Zuleikha by Guzel Yakhina (Russian)
Translated by Lisa C. Hayden

Mouthful of Birds by Samanta Schweblin (Spanish)
Translated by Megan McDowell

City of Jasmine by Olga Grjasnowa (German)
Translated by Katy Derbyshire

Things that Fall from the Sky by Selja Ahava (Finnish)
Translated by Emily Jeremiah and Fleur Jeremiah

Mrs Mohr Goes Missing by Maryla Szymiczkowa (Polish)
Translated by Antonia Lloyd-Jones

In the Shadow of Wolves by Alvydas Šlepikas (Lithuanian)
Translated by Romas Kinka

Humiliation by Paulina Flores (Spanish)
Translated by Megan McDowell

Paulina Flores was born in Chile in 1988. In 2014, she won the Roberto Bolaño Short Story Prize for her story 'Qué vergüenza' ('Humiliation'), and her collection of the same title was published to great acclaim in Chile the following year. She is a laureate of the Chilean Art Critics Circle Prize for Best New Fiction. *Humiliation* is her first book, and was selected as one of the ten best books of 2016 by *El País* newspaper.

Megan McDowell has translated books by many contemporary South American and Spanish authors, including Samanta Schweblin's Man Booker International-shortlisted *Fever Dream*. Her translations have been published in *The New Yorker*, *Harper's* and *The Paris Review*. She lives in Chile.